LOST-IN-PETRA

For Mom and Dad - K
For Hana - M

Text copyright © 2012 SpyGirls Press
Cover illustration © 2012 Jeff James
Interior illustrations © 2012 SpyGirls Press

SpyGirls Press
P.O. Box 1537
Fairfax, VA 22038
Visit our website at www.anatoliasteppe.com
First Edition: April 2012

The characters and events portrayed in this book are fictitious.
Any similarity to real persons, living or dead, is coincidental
and not intended by the authors.

Library of Congress Cataloging-in-Publication Data
Mahle, Melissa and Dennis, Kathryn
Lost in Petra/Melissa Mahle and Kathryn Dennis;
Cover Illustration by Jeff James

1st ed. P. cm. – (Anatolia Steppe Mystery Series, Book One)
Summary: Eleven-year old Anatolia Steppe arrives in Petra, Jordan
and discovers her mother missing. In the search to find her and the
fabled Horde of the Golden Girdle, Ana befriends a boy named Gordy.
Together they track tomb robbers, uncover a spy and discover much
more than gold and silver.
ISBN — 978-0-9852273-0-2
[1. Mysteries & Detective – Fiction. 2. Action & Adventure –
Fiction. 3. Legends, Myths & Fables – Fiction.]
Library of Congress Control Number: 2012904905

ANATOLIA ☾ STEPPE

LOST–IN–PETRA

MELISSA MAHLE AND KATHRYN DENNIS

WHERE TRUTH AND FALSEHOOD
TWIST AND TURN.
BE CAREFUL OF WHO YOU TRUST.
AND WHO YOU DO NOT.
ALL IS NOT AS IT SEEMS.

spygirls press

CONTENTS

PROLOGUE

Kingdom of Petra; 40 AD

Queen Huldu kneels before the feet of the winged statue. She holds the Golden Girdle, the greatest treasure of the Nabatean people. She prays.

"Oh Greatest Goddess of my people and the Kingdom of Petra, Most Powerful 'Uzza, protect us from our enemies who seek to destroy us."

The Queen raises the golden object studded with jewels higher as she looks through the open roof of the temple to the blue-white desert sky and the tops of the Red Mountains. She trembles.

"Oh Greatest Goddess 'Uzza, curse those who seek to steal our treasures."

The Queen reaches for the round amulet hanging at her neck. "Protect this key to the Map of the Gods. Let only those who seek to honor us escape your curse."

The sound of horses and men's voices ring out. Salome, sent as a spy by her brother King Herod, would soon arrive. Then the Roman legions of war.

A twist of fate would keep Queen Huldu from knowing her prayers had been heard. Petra would fall, first to the swords of the Romans and then to the forces of a devastating earthquake. Petra's secrets would be buried, and over time it would be forgotten.

For two thousand years.

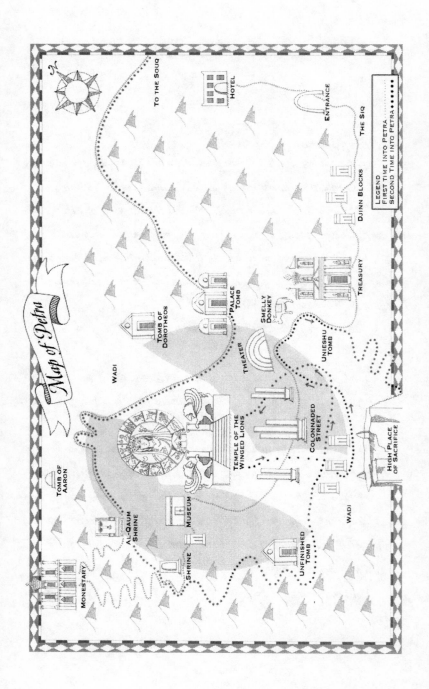

Map of Petra

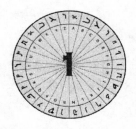

A Slick Man and
an Unwelcome Message

I never thought a puzzle would cause me so much trouble. I'm really good at puzzles. I can see the shapes in my mind and put them in their proper order while most people are still just gathering up their pieces. I remember other things too. Names, places, and pieces of languages from all my travels. They swirl around in my head until I need to find an answer, and then I pluck them from my memory on command.

But this puzzle is different.

Using one of my braids, I swing for the third time at a fly with a death wish. I arrived in the Kingdom of Jordan over fourteen hours ago, and there's still no sign of my mom. I gave up waiting in her room, and I've taken to staking out the lobby. She has a tendency to forget about everything, me included, when she's working. There are lots of black- and brown-haired women, even a couple of redheads like me, but I don't see Mom's blonde ponytail anywhere.

I squeeze my backpack, which I'm using as a chin rest, and keep my eyes glued on the revolving glass doors that rotate people in and out of the Mövenpick Resort Petra. I'm holding my backpack tight for a reason. Buried deep under my journal and my prized box of colored pencils is a secret wrapped in muslin. The mailman delivered it to our New York brownstone yesterday just before the taxi arrived to take us to the airport. It's part of a puzzle too, a mysterious one. But because it's a secret, I first have to lose the Brownlet, aka Gordy Brown.

Gordy is heading across the lobby looking for me at this very moment. I didn't know my new nanny Mrs. Brown had a kid until yesterday. Why do grownups think just because you're the same age, you have anything in common? The quick grin and bright eyes might be cute to some. But I'm no sucker. Mom can force Mrs. Brown on me, but no one's going to make Gordy my friend.

I drop down behind the back of the gold and red sofa I've been perched on while waiting for Mom—who is now fourteen hours, thirty-two minutes late—and hide from Gordy. The lobby is the size of my school gym, with a giant revolving door to freedom. Lucky for me the lobby is packed with tourists, piles of luggage and one crazy guide waving a stick with a yellow flag attached. I couldn't have planned a better distraction.

I dart across the marble tiles and take cover behind a suitcase large enough to hold me. I peek around the expensive leather and spot Gordy's blond head. He's looking in the other direction. My eyes sweep the room, searching for Mrs. Brown. I do not need a nanny. I'm eleven and very mature for my age. She's more like a spy or prison guard. I plan on ditching her real soon.

A wailing echoes from outside the hotel, drowning out the chatter of the lobby. A second voice joins the wailer, and then a third and a fourth, chanting in rounds. I know from all my trips to the Middle East that the voices are calling the people to the mosques for prayer. It's like Grand Central Station at home, with different loudspeakers announcing the departure of trains, one cutting the other off so you can't understand what track your train is leaving from, but you know you'd better get moving or you'll be late.

I clutch my backpack tighter and head for a potted palm half way between Gordy and the exit. Since Mom's either really late or forgot I exist again, I'll just have to track her down myself. How hard can that be?

I bolt for the automatic revolving door planning to make my escape. There are glass sections, almost like a pie cut into three pieces. It moves at a set speed, so slow I have to take baby steps once I'm in to keep from running into the glass in front of me. A sweaty man rushes into the section on the other side of me,

3

heading into the hotel. His dark shiny suit seems to change shape as he moves. He motions to me, hands on the glass and his lips move, but I can't hear a thing he's saying.

When his section reaches the opening to the lobby, he swings himself around the glass barrier, and squeezes into my section. His cologne overpowers the small space. There is nowhere to go; I am trapped by metal and glass.

"Miss Anatolia? Miss Steppe?" Mr. Shiny Pants asks in the clipped vowels of proper English.

I cringe. No one calls me Anatolia unless they want to be on my enemy list forever. Forever means for–ever. Only Mom gets away with it and only when I'm in serious trouble.

"It's just Ana." I throw my body weight against the glass hoping to make it move faster. The door refuses to hurry.

"Why are you here? Did you not receive Dr. Steppe's fax?" He struggles to catch his breath. A large bead of sweat slides from the hairline to the pencil moustache lining his top lip.

"My mom's expecting me." I blot out the memory of the fax on Mövenpick Resort stationary that I destroyed before coming here.

"The fax advised you not to come." Mr. Shiny Pants flicks a red silk handkerchief from his breast pocket and smoothes his hair. It looks as though he's used the same jet-black polish on his hair as his shoes.

Fax machines, like dinosaurs, are extinct. Except in Mom's world. Communication with Mom is always a problem. Not counting the fax—which I'm not admitting to have seen—or the secret package—which I'm not admitting exists—I haven't received a single email or phone call from her since she left for Petra two weeks ago. She often goes places where indoor plumbing is a luxury and the Internet is unheard of. Once I received a telegram, which is about as ancient a communication system as sending smoke signals. Between the mountains and the lack of reception, I can forget about my cell phone working here in Petra.

Now I put all my weight against the glass door and push harder. Five more inches until freedom. But instead of moving faster, the door jerks to a stop.

"*Ya Allah,*" Mr. Shiny Pants says as he runs into me, his attention on the figures inside. "What has happened?"

I look back into the hotel lobby. There's Gordy, his long blond bangs in his eyes, waving his arms like a wild man. His mouth moves nonstop. Jammed between the revolving door and the wall is the padded strap of his backpack. The doorman is pulling on the strap. It is wedged tight, refusing to budge and release the door. I hear a metallic groan as the motor running the door strains.

Great. Now Gordy's trapped me.

"What a shambles!" Mr. Shiny Pants flaps his red kerchief toward me before tucking it back in his pocket, showing off trimmed and polished nails. "Where is Mrs. Brown? I must speak with her at once."

I give him my sweetest smile. "She's been kidnapped by Arabian thieves."

Mr. Shiny Pants jerks his head back, the left side of the mustache twitching. "Your nanny has disappeared?"

"I'm working on it," I assure him. I would gladly give up my allowance for an entire year just to make sure it happened.

He glares at me, smoothing his mustache. "I will arrange for your immediate return. There's a government airport in Petra. You can travel by helicopter back to Amman and arrive in time to catch the evening flight to New York."

The door releases with a loud groan of the gears and begins to rotate again. I see the doorman holding the backpack up in the air while herding Gordy away from the door. I press on the glass, breathing in the fresh air as the opening grows inch by inch. "I'm not leaving until I see my mom."

"I'm sorry but that is not possible." Before I can slip through the opening, Mr. Shiny Pants grabs my elbow. I struggle but his grip is too strong. He steers me back into the noisy lobby, releasing me only when I am safely inside.

"I don't take orders from strangers!" I shout. Tourists stop and stare.

Mr. Shiny Pants frowns. "Forgive me." He reaches inside his jacket for a slim silver case and removes a business card. "Allow me to properly introduce myself. I am Mr. Hasan, Deputy Minister of Antiquities. It is Dr. Steppe's wish that you return home. Immediately. She does not have time for you."

It's as if he's plunged one of those curved daggers hanging on the wall above the reception desk into my heart and twisted it. "You're a liar."

Sweat is dripping down his face, but his words freeze the air between us. "I am many things, young lady, but I assure you that your well-being is my highest priority. Dangers lurk outside these walls that you cannot imagine. I am only protecting you."

"Yeah, right," I say with a snort.

A STINKY GIFT AND
A NOSY NANNY

Mr. Shiny Pants heads to the front desk to page Mrs. Brown. I fling myself into an overstuffed chair tucked in the corner of the lobby behind the palm tree. It is out of sight of the tourists, the front desk and Gordy, who is still being lectured by the doorman. I study Mr. Hasan's business card through blurry eyes. The seal of the Ministry of Antiquities is embossed in the upper-left corner. I rub the raised print; it doesn't come off. When I hold the card up to the light the paper gleams. I figure that means Mr. Hasan is for real. It makes me hate him even more.

I wind my braids around my neck like a scarf and chew one end. I dab my eyes with the other tip. My hair falls below my waist now. Mom promised there would be no haircuts as long as I kept it under control. This was supposed to be *my* trip with her. She can't cancel me. She promised.

If this were the first time, I might be nice about it. But it's not. Ever since Dad disappeared six months ago, she's worked late almost every night. I let the dishes pile up in the sink and left my clothes on the floor, hoping she'd notice, which only got me a nanny, not Mom.

Checking again to make sure no one is watching, I pull out the secret package Mom sent. Unwinding the cloth wrapping, I run my fingers over the lumpy surface of what looks to be ancient cow pie. Smells like one too. I also pull out the enclosed picture of a statue, a woman holding a large disk over her head. It looks like Mom tore it out of a magazine or a museum catalogue. In the bright light of the lobby, I notice something I missed when I first opened the package at home: faint pencil markings in the white margin around the picture. I've seen those patterns somewhere before but my brain is playing ping-pong right now, and I'm not in the mood for Match-That-Scribble. I re-read Mom's note, the biggest puzzle of all.

Yavrum—Protect this. It points the way to the GG. If I am detained, beware of the imposter.
Love, Mom

An ancient sun disk the Nabatean's ... map
the celestial ... r. ...in the Temple of the
...ged Lions.

11

It's Mom's handwriting, but it doesn't sound like her. For one thing, she used my secret name. *Yavrum,* Turkish for "little animal." Only Dad used that name, never Mom. Maybe she's been working in the sun without her hat, and her brains got cooked. 98 degrees is considered a cool day in Petra. As for the meaning of GG—

"Whatcha got there?"

I spring up, sending my backpack flying. I hurry to hide Mom's secret from the prying blue eyes of Gordy Brown.

"Get lost." I wrap the cloth over everything and shove it back into my pack. Gordy seems to have a problem understanding personal space. Privacy. All the stuff that's important to me. "It's nothing." I hug my backpack.

"It's definitely something."

"It's a gift from my mom." Then I flare my nostrils. How am I supposed to protect mom's secret if Mr. Blabbermouth finds out about it and tells the whole world? He spent our entire flight and the long car ride from Amman to Petra talking to anyone who would listen. Then I have a terrible thought. What if Mrs. Brown brings him along every time she travels with Mom and me? I'm hoping this trip together is an exception, a special occasion, or just a freak accident. "Shouldn't you be with your mom?"

"There you two are," Mrs. Brown says, walking up behind Gordy.

Ugh. I'm totally jinxed. One word about Mrs. Brown, and she appears. If it really is Mrs. Brown. She's wearing an oversized straw hat that cups down over her face and shoulders, hiding her blonde hair. Dark sunglasses cover her eyes, so all I can see are her lips and nose. I prefer her covered up because this way I can't see how much she resembles Mom.

Mrs. Brown sniffs the air. "Gordy put on clean clothes. Did you?"

I look at Gordy. If I were Mrs. Brown, I wouldn't brag. He's dressed in shorts and a T-shirt with sharp creases that scream brand new, and he has the whitest legs I've ever seen. His red sneakers are spotless. Either they're just out of the box or this kid's a super freak. I sniff my shirt and decide it can make it another day or two. Same for my favorite jeans, the ones with a hole in the left knee from the time I tried to climb an apple tree to get on my cousin's roof and missed, big time. I cut them off just above my knees before I left for Jordan, and I plan on wearing them the entire time. Or until Mom confiscates them.

"I wanted to find my mom first."

"And did you?"

I feel Mrs. Brown's eyes on me from behind the sunglasses. I twirl a braid trying to buy some time. She wouldn't be asking if she'd already talked to Mr. Hasan. Unless it's a trap. I search the lobby but don't see Mr. Hasan. There's no way I'm telling her about his plan to send us home. Or his asking about the missing fax. She'd suspect me in a nanosecond.

"She's still working."

"Is she?" Mrs. Brown's lips form a tight smile. "Your mother's work is important. It doesn't mean she doesn't love you."

"I know," I shoot back. "She's really sorry she's late."

"Is that why she gave you the present?" Gordy asks.

If looks could kill, he'd be flat on the marble tile right now. Why can't he keep his fat mouth closed?

"What present?" Mrs. Brown asks.

"Can I see?" Gordy asks.

"It's personal." I clutch the strap of my backpack tighter.

Mrs. Brown sighs. "Why don't you give me your room key and your pack? It looks awfully heavy. I'll unpack and organize your belongings after lunch. Then you can shower and change." Mrs. Brown peers at me over the top of her sunglasses. There's no mistaking the laser blue eyes now.

That's the other thing about Mrs. Brown; she's a neat freak. Even more than Mom. Since she started working for us, she's been through every drawer and closet, organizing as she calls it. Disorganizing is more like it, since I can't find anything.

I feel a clench deep down in my stomach. It's much more than the bag of gummy worms I ate on the plane. I think of Dad's Rules. Dad always said when my gut talks to me, I should

14

listen. That's rule number two. Rule number one is safety. Mr. Hasan said it was dangerous outside the hotel, but I've traveled all over the world from the day I was born. The way Mrs. Brown is eyeing my bag, I'd say staying in this hotel could be dangerous.

I chew the end of one of my braids as a bell dings, jumbling my thoughts. A bellboy walks through the lobby, holding a small slate sign high overhead, deafening the guests with a bell to get their attention. I see "Madame Brown" in large chalk letters. My heart sinks. Mr. Hasan must be paging her. Time to ditch the Browns.

"Lunch? Hotel buffets will kill you. It's not safe," I announce. Dad's number one rule, safety first. "Later," I shout. "Don't let the sand fleas bite." I run for the revolving doors. I see freedom just as Gordy's foot catches the back of my sneaker and gives me a flat tire.

"Wait!" Gordy yells.

I don't stop, but shake my shoe to pop it back on.

Gordy throws himself in front of the revolving door, arms spread to keep me from getting by. I'm determined not to let him stop me this time. The only option is to tackle him. He's taller than me, but I'm skinnier. When a sliver of an opening appears, I break loose from him and squeeze past into the blistering air of the Jordanian summer. I have a mom to find.

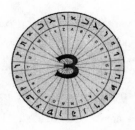

A Young Guide and
a Tomb Robber

The afternoon sun reflects off the stone buildings, making my eyeballs sizzle. Dust and discarded plastic shopping bags swirl in the hot wind, attacking my ankles. I sprint across the road in front of the hotel, forcing a car to swerve. Men hang out the windows, and two boys and a sheep are perched on the roof rack.

"What happened to being safe?" Gordy yells, waiting for the traffic to clear before catching up to me.

"Safe is for sissies." I glance at the map of Petra I found in my hotel room. Petra is divided into two parts: the archeological park, home of the Nabateans, long dead, and the Jordanian town of Wadi Musa, still living. Mom's probably somewhere in the archaeological part, but I'll have an easier time losing Mrs. Brown in the *souq* if she decides to try and follow me. I ignore Gordy who's listing the pros and cons of going off on our own, like I haven't already made that decision.

I turn left for the modern town. The buildings are hand cut from stone, blasted smooth by the wind and desert sand. I can make out a few domes against the pale sky, but they appear more dusty than gold. The spiraling minarets topped with orbs and crescent moons catch the sunlight and look like the work of genies. Arched doors, twice as tall as normal, make me wonder if people still enter their homes on horseback. Even the trees are aged by sand. They call this modern?

I see what I'm searching for in between two domed buildings: a double archway. I take the stone steps leading down into the market by twos. On the last step, I'm transported back in time. The street noise, with the honking of cars, disappears and is replaced by the braying of a donkey pulling a cart and shopkeepers calling out in broken English, "Welcome shop please" and "Special deal Americans." The latticework overhead filters the sun, and the air feels cooler.

Narrow shops line the alley as it winds through the marketplace. I walk faster, my skin tingling. From doorways hang embroidered dresses for women, silk scarves, throw rugs and wooden carvings. Shelves are piled with brass pots and plates, pottery and carvings. People and animals move with no clear pattern in the traffic like Times Square on New Year's Eve. Plastic bags and paper litter the walkway. I push through the crowd, using my elbows to clear a path. Thoughts of Dad fill my head, and I can't push them away. He should be here. We always explored the markets together and talked to people in the towns and villages while Mom would be lost to the living world at some dig site. Now he's lost to me. I try not to think about him, but I miss him more than anything in the world— no, the universe. I wish Dad were here instead of the annoying Gordy. I pass a café and fill my lungs with the aromas. I'd tell Dad it's the best smell ever: week-old socks mixed with freshly ground coffee and magic. Gordy probably thinks it just stinks.

"Why are those men wearing dresses?" Gordy points at a group of Arabs in white *jalabiyas* huddled around a table drinking coffee from doll-size cups.

I snort when a rhyme pops into my head. *Oh momma-mia don't you love that jala-biya.* Dad taught it to me to help me with the pronunciation. I love how he always knew about the people and what to say to make them like us. We'd sit at the outdoor cafes, and he'd point out how the color of the *kiffiyahs* the men wore around their necks or on their head told what tribe they came from, some all white, others red-and-white or black-and-white checkered. He'd greet them differently, and they liked that. Dad said it was like knowing when to say good-morning or howdy when making a new friend. Sometimes the men would sit with us, or invite us to their homes for lunch or show off their families and herds. Dad made friends every place he went.

"Those are their regular clothes."

A woman in a black robe down to her ankles, hair hidden under a scarf, thrusts a piece of paper at me. I take it. A boy, maybe twelve years old, smiles up at me from the page. From my travels, I've picked up more than ten words in ten languages, including Arabic. So I thank her with a *shukran*. I wonder why the lady's eyes look so sad. I wish I knew the right words to ask what the squiggly script under the boy's picture says. I can order food, ask directions and bargain, but I haven't yet learned to read Arabic.

"Isn't she hot?" Gordy stares at lady's heavy black clothes.

"Keep staring and she'll think you're giving her the evil eye." What is it with this kid and all the questions? Hasn't he ever traveled?

Gordy turns away and smacks into a passing cart. I have to grab him by his shirt to pull him out of the path of the wooden wheels. I seriously do not have the time to babysit him.

A dusty boy tugs on my arm. "You need guide? Dangerous walk souq alone." He lowers his voice and adds, "Kids not safe. Bad men steal kids. No come back."

"But you're a kid." I laugh away his warning. Just because he's a head taller than me doesn't mean he has my experience traveling the back alleys of the world. I am impressed he speaks English, and a lot better than I speak Arabic. I'm not planning on admitting that to him or Gordy.

The boy gives a slight bow. "I am guide. I keep safe over you and show Petra souq. One hundred dollars American."

"My mother warned me about scammers who—" Gordy says.

"That is me." The boy smiles, smacking his chest with his fist. His teeth are crooked and grey. He doesn't look like he flosses. Mom might have a point. "I am Faisal, best guide in Petra. My father born here, and my father's father, and his father. I know every rock."

"Are you crazy? A hundred dollars?" Gordy says.

"Will you take us wherever we want to go? No questions asked?" I glare at Gordy.

"Anywhere. Yes?"

"We don't have a hundred dollars," Gordy warns.

Faisal bows again, a sly grin visible for a moment before his red-and-white kiffiyah hides his face. I know this trick. He wants me to haggle with him until we agree on a price to close the deal.

"Twenty dollars. All day. The two of us," I offer.

"Eighty dollar."

"Twenty-one."

"Fifty dollar. Only four hour. Yes?"

"Twenty-five. All day."

"*Tayib,*" Faisal says. "I get you special deal in souq."

"You promised you'd take me wherever I wanted."

"Souq first, then anywhere. Yes?"

21

"I was thinking we should wait. My mother's going to be angry if we go without her." Gordy looks around.

Tayib, I tell Faisal. Deal. There's no way I'm going back to the hotel and let Mr. Hasan send me home.

Faisal guides us deep into the souq, greeting shopkeepers as we pass and promising to return to their shops later. There's no way Mrs. Brown can find us now. I notice Gordy is counting steps. It must be his way of dropping breadcrumbs. I'm not worried. Dad always called me his personal GPS; I never get lost. It's my secret weapon when playing my favorite board game. Players have to move from one side of the board to the other, interlocking geometric figures based on shapes and colors to win. Even Dad couldn't beat me.

"How long have you been a guide?" Gordy asks Faisal.

Faisal holds up his thumb and five fingers.

"Years? No way! What about school?" Gordy asks.

"No, six moons. Done with school. Faisal works."

Six months? I'm surprised. Faisal doesn't look more than thirteen or fourteen. If I said I was quitting school after the seventh grade, Mom would run me through her shredder and then stuff me down the garbage disposal.

"I help family so little brother learn at good school. British school. Ali smart. He make famous engineer. He make bridge to America!" Faisal smiles, showing off his crooked teeth at the mention of Ali.

22

"Your parents are okay that you don't go to school?"

"God preserve them." Faisal places his hand across his heart. "They are dead. My father's father begin me as guide."

"At least you *have* family," Gordy says in a way that makes me look at him. He's frowning. I wonder if he's part orphan like me. But I don't say anything because he'll just start jabbering. I'm not in the mood to hear him go on about his entire family tree since the days of the Mayflower. I want to know about one person.

"Have you seen a blonde American woman around the last few weeks? She's working with the Ministry of Antiquities."

Faisal shakes his head. "I not know. But I show you office of Ministry. You ask there. Yes?"

I shake my head because I'm thinking Mr. Shiny Pants is probably there issuing orders to travel agents, helicopter pilots, air traffic control and anybody else who will listen to him.

"My mom works for a big American museum. She's putting together a traveling exhibition of rare Nabatean stuff."

Faisal looks impressed so it's my turn to stand a little taller. Mom has an important job, tracking down old artifacts and recreating the stories of lost civilizations.

"Have you ever heard about the Golden Girdle?" I ask.

"Famous lost treasure of Nabateans."

I suck in my breath. He knows about the Golden Girdle too?

"There's a missing treasure?" Gordy cuts in between Faisal and me to listen in as we walk through the crowd of shoppers.

"Horde of Golden Girdle," Faisal says to Gordy. "Gold and jewels. Treasure of Nabatean kings and queens."

"Where is it?" Gordy says.

I frown. I don't want Gordy getting interested in the Golden Girdle. "It's just a legend."

Faisal motions his hand toward the lattice roof over our heads. "Red mountains hide secrets."

I'm beginning to think we should have gone with a licensed guide. One who can give more specific information. "Have you heard of anyone finding any clues?"

"We go to nice shop. Shopkeeper knows all about Nabateans. Yes?"

Faisal stops in front of a doorway with a carpet serving as the door. The sign says Sinbad Souvenirs. The shop must be magical because the skinny door opens into a room almost as large as the hotel lobby. The walls, ceilings and floor are covered with textiles and brass, one hundred different shades of reds, blues, greens and golds; it's brain overload to take it all in. Baskets of beads and stones coated with grime cover the tables. It's a trick to make me pay more for something old. But I'm not buying.

I'm knee deep in rolled carpets and overturned copper pots trying to decide how to get the shop owner to tell me about the

Golden Girdle without my asking, when the bells hanging alongside the doorway jingle. I smell perspiration mixed with spicy aftershave first, and then I hear a man with a clipped English accent greet the shopkeeper. He's short and wiry and moves like a terrier after a mouse. He picks items up and makes of show of announcing to the world what they are, the period they come from and whether they're real or fake, acting like he's an expert and wants everyone to know it. He wears a white suit with an open collar shirt. At first I wonder if he's an archeologist, but then I decide white doesn't go with people who spend most of their time digging in the dirt. I creep along the rolls of carpet and peer around a table of statues. Gordy motions toward the door, but I shake my head. I'm interested in this customer.

The man approaches the shopkeeper in a white jalabiya who is resting his elbows on a glass display case.

"I've heard rumors that a fragment of a Goddess 'Uzza statue was found of late in Petra," the man says. He keeps his voice low, like he doesn't want the flies to overhear.

The shopkeeper stifles a yawn and pulls himself up. He smiles, forcing his lips apart, revealing a gold tooth. "English?" he asks. I've seen this game before. Dad says never let on you're interested.

"Scottish, my good fellow. A mutual friend suggested you might know where I could obtain something like this." He pulls an envelope out of the pocket of his jacket. "There's a good sum of money in it for you." He unfolds a piece of paper and hands it to the merchant.

I smother a gasp by chomping on my braid. No archaeologist would offer money for a real artifact. I stare at the man. This is my first encounter with a tomb robber. That's what Mom calls collectors of stolen artifacts. They're no better than the thieves who break into museums in the middle of the night. I inch toward the tomb robber.

"I believe I can help you. I heard a similar piece was found in the Temple of the Winged Lions." The shopkeeper strokes his baldhead. "Come back tomorrow."

Tomb Robber thanks the shopkeeper and places the folded paper back in the envelope. He hesitates for a moment and takes his handkerchief out of his other jacket pocket. "I have recently acquired this piece and wonder if it is one of a kind, or if you've seen others like it?" The man unwraps the cloth, and I catch sight of a flash of gold. I inch forward for a better look.

The shopkeeper's mouth drops open, and then he snaps it shut, trying to look bored again. But I can tell he's interested. He redirects the light of a small lamp on the counter, illuminating the gold piece. Is it a coin? It looks too big. I step over a carpet and peek out from behind a wooden post.

"A lion?" the shopkeeper asks. Tomb Robber nods, not taking his eyes off the shopkeeper.

The shopkeeper licks his lips. He tries to take the gold piece, but Tomb Robber pulls it back out of his reach. "Have you seen such a piece before?" There's a slippery tone to his voice, like when Mrs. Brown wants to know where Mom keeps something.

"Many years ago a piece like this was found. Not with a lion, but a crab."

"Where is it now?"

"Petra Museum."

"So I cannot acquire it?"

The man licks his lips again. "It would be difficult."

"Difficult or impossible?"

"If it is wished, I make inquiries." The shopkeeper's eyes narrow on the handkerchief hiding the gold piece.

"What is it? My research informs me it is not coinage. Perhaps a ceremonial piece?"

"I do not know for certain. They say the crab disk is of great value and is part of the Horde of the Golden Girdle."

Tomb Robber flashes with excitement. "You are most helpful. Discreet inquires only. May I bother you with one last affair?" He slides a few coins across the counter and takes a photo out of the envelope. "I'd be interested if you've seen this woman. Rival collector, if you know what I mean."

My eye catches a flash of color and shapes. Blonde ponytail, sharp nose. Mom?

The shopkeeper clicks his tongue, no in Arabic.

I slip around the post, but the photo is gone before I can get a second look. A rival collector? That can't be Mom.

When Tomb Robber slides the envelope back into his jacket pocket, I notice a silver snakehead winding its way around his middle finger. I'm not a fan of snakes. I don't care if they are plastic, gummy, or silver. There's only one thing I hate more than snakes, and that's a scorpion. Just the thought of them makes me shudder so hard my head clips the edge of a copper pot hanging on the wooden post. It's like a row of dominos when the rest of the pots begin crashing down around me. I screech and jump out of the way, knocking Tomb Robber into a table packed with trays of stones, sending them flying across the carpeted floor.

The shopkeeper apologizes over and over again to the man, helping him up from the floor and dusting off his now not-so-perfect suit. Tomb Robber looks right at me, and I swear he growls. His stiff, wiry hair stands on end, like he might bite any minute. Then the shopkeeper starts screaming at me in Arabic. I don't have to know all the words to get what he is saying. Faisal springs from his perch by the door and is bowing, his hand over his heart. Despite the chaos, my eyes lock on the envelope that has landed on the floor. Lucky for me, Tomb Robber doesn't notice. He just glowers at me as he marches out of the shop.

The three of us flee to the alley. My eyes are still adjusting to the light, as I am caught in a knot of shoppers, battering me one way and then the other until I find a corner out of the way of traffic. I rummage through my pocket for the envelope; I'm certain it's an important clue to something. But what?

An Eyeball and
a Litterbug

"Wonder why he didn't have you arrested?" Gordy slides in beside me out of the mob of shoppers.

"Why don't you go back and find out."

Faisal keeps looking over his shoulder at the shop. "We walk now. Yes?"

I ignore them both and the chattering of the market. Sitting on the doorstep of a closed shop, I yank the piece of paper from its envelope and see Tomb Robber's secret: a giant eyeball. The words below the drawing read, Alabaster Eye of 'Uzza.

"What's that?" Gordy sticks his finger in the middle of the eye.

I whip the drawing out of his reach, angry that Gordy is still here. "The eyeball of someone called 'Uzza."

"Nabatean people worship Goddess 'Uzza. This before knowing Allah and the Prophet, peace be upon Him. 'Uzza head goddess."

Faisal might be an okay guide after all.

"They prayed to an eyeball?" Gordy says.

"You've never read about gods and goddesses? Greek, Roman, whatever, they all have their own symbols. Like New York and the Big Apple, or your school mascot."

I imagine a giant, fuzzy eyeball leading the school assembly at Marymount Academy for Girls. Then I realize we have one: Principal Frost, minus the fuzzy part.

"But why does that man want it?"

"He's a tomb robber, stealing the past from everybody, so it's lost forever."

"Isn't that what archaeologists do? Like your mother?" Gordy says.

"Take it back." I crumple the edge of the drawing in irritation. "My mom doesn't steal. Archeologists can't keep what they find."

Gordy looks back at the paper in my hand, eyebrows arched in disbelief. "They can keep some stuff though, right?"

"Not even broken pottery. Museums have first dibs." I snort, unable to believe anyone is this dumb.

"But my mother's house is full—" Gordy stops, his ears turning pink on the tips. He removes his pack of cards out of his pocket and starts shuffling. He flips over the card on the top of the deck: three of diamonds. He makes a show of putting it back in the deck, shuffles, cuts the deck in half and shows me the same red card. He then fans out five cards. "Pick any card. I bet I can tell you what it is. Nine out of ten times I'm right. It's just practice. I'm not supposed to tell how I do it, but if you want, I can teach you."

"I don't want to play now." What I really mean is I don't want to play ever.

When I don't drool at his talent, he asks, "Why an eyeball?"

"Maybe Tomb Robber hopes it will tell him where the treasure is hidden. Kind of like the Magic 8 Ball."

Gordy grins. "Are we looking for a treasure?"

We who? He's wrong if he thinks we're going to be friends. I don't care if he's a poker grand champion or that Sarah would say Gordy's cute even with knobby knees. Sarah's my former BFF. Former because she abandoned me by moving to Florida.

I unzip my backpack, and the smell of cinnamon and dung wafts out. Then I have a bad thought. If Mom can't keep what she finds, why is this package stinking up my bag? Her note said it would show the way to the GG. She has to mean the Golden Girdle. The cow pie doesn't look like much but it'd be pretty valuable if led to the discovery of an ancient treasure. Maybe Tomb Robber did have Mom's picture, and they're after the same thing? If so, he's getting a head start while Mom is working.

Despite Faisal's constant pacing and pestering to get going, I settle into a more comfortable position on some steps, leaning against the shutters of a closed shop. I take out my journal and box of colored pencils. At least Dad's presents to me don't stink. The pencils, a Valentine from Dad, are almost new. I press the tip of my finger against a sharp point. It's the last thing he gave me. I draw with them only in my journal so they will last forever. Once I use them up, then Dad will be gone.

I pull out the charcoal pencil and begin to copy the drawing while Gordy shuffles cards in my ear. Even though the original is done in black ink, I decide 'Uzza needs some color. I select the mint green pencil and fill in the iris. Mom has green eyes, although not as minty. I wonder for a moment if Mom's eyes are magical, and she can see treasures hidden in the ground. I wish she could see inside my heart. She wouldn't want to send me away then. If she has to work, I could help her.

My pencil stops. I could help. I have an important clue. I can make sure Tomb Robber doesn't get to the Golden Girdle first.

I stuff my journal into my pack and look for Tomb Robber's envelope. That's when I notice a store advertisement on the ground between my feet. The card must have fallen out when I opened the envelope. Why would Tomb Robber be interested in a fortuneteller? I keep the card and crumple up the envelope, paper and all, tossing them into the walkway.

Gordy lunges off the step into the path of shoppers. "That's littering."

"No worry, Mr. Gordy," Faisal says. "Street sweeper"

"I'm not littering, I'm disposing of evidence. If Tomb Robber comes looking for it, he'll think he dropped it."

Gordy's shakes his head like Principal Frost does when I talk in the hallway. He shoves the envelope in his backpack.

"People think one piece of paper can't hurt, but one here, one there." He grabs more garbage off ground. "Next we're living in a trash pile."

He springs at a thin black plastic bag drifting in the breeze, tangling between the legs of shoppers. The current licks it up, out of his reach, as it soars overhead, up and out of the souq. "Did you know plastic bags are choking the earth? It takes like a billion years for them to biodegrade. We can't keep throwing things away."

I hate lectures, especially from a kid branding me a litterbug. I protest my innocence, saying there are no trash cans, but Faisal butts in, alarm in his voice.

"We go now. Yes? Right now?"

The shopkeeper from Sinbad Souvenirs stands in the alley, pointing at us. Next to him is a policeman dressed in a dark green uniform. The policeman is as wide as he is tall. He holds a strand of worry beads in his left hand, flicking one marble-size bead at a time with his flat thumbnail. Our eyes meet. Above the clamor of the souq, I hear his nail clack against the bead, like a fist against my stomach.

We scramble down the pathway and around a corner, but I wouldn't call it super sneaky because I have a giggle attack, like a twitch I can't stop when I'm nervous. I've been in Petra for less than a day, and already I'm a fugitive and a litterbug.

Faisal's not laughing. "We shop better place. Nice owner. No police. Yes?"

I hold the shop card I took from Tomb Robber. "I want to go to Madam Isis's Tea Reading Shoppe."

Faisal crosses his forefingers in front of his face as if to block out my words. "You not waste money with fortuneteller." He wheels around and strides toward the entrance of a shop full of old maps and drawings.

I dig in my heels. "I want to see Madam Isis."

"Miss Ana, fortuneteller house of *djinn*. Bad luck."

"You promised you'd take me wherever I wanted."

Gordy laughs. "What are you going to learn from a lady guzzling gin and drooling on a crystal ball? Bet she'd see a pink camel with three humps in your future."

"Djinn, evil spirits. Play mean tricks." Faisal shoots Gordy a look.

I'm giving Gordy my best evil eye look when it backfires. A soccer ball hits me smack on the top of my head. Hard. It bounces off, and a boy catches it with his foot, flips it up toward his shoulder where he rolls it back down his arm. He grins at me as he runs by. Figures a soccer ball would bean me. It's the one sport every fifth grader at my school who doesn't want to be labeled a loser plays, and the one I'm a complete failure at. Since I've already had my share of bad luck today, I figure a reading could be useful. Plus, how can I pass up a chance to meet a real live fortuneteller.

"Take me to Madam Isis or I'll find her on my own." I clutch the strap of my backpack and turn back into the depths of the souq. My instincts scream Madam Isis has answers, or at least Tomb Robber thinks so.

I launch into the stream of shoppers, dodging oncoming traffic. A pair of new red sneakers and two tattered sandals slap the stone walkway behind me.

A Queen and a Spirit

We plunge back into darkness as we enter Madam Isis's Tea Readings Shoppe. I push through veils of fabric to an inner room where incense overpowers the small space. Gordy holds his nose and fakes gagging. The walls are covered with Persian rugs. Crimson designs weave like vines, looping and twisting, connecting one carpet to the next. In the candlelight the carpets seem to move, snaking along the walls and deadening the air.

"Hello?" My voice is muted by the thick carpets.

"I gotta get out of here before I barf." Gordy squeezes his nose.

I love the scent of sandalwood, so I try to ignore Gordy, but the hairs on the back of my neck prickle. I start to turn back when I see a women materialize in front of one of the rugs. She seems to walk right out of the wall. I shake my head, but there's a real woman standing in front of me. She's dressed in robes of red and gold matching the rug.

"Seventeen dinars for a half hour. I tell your fortune or we speak to a dead relative. You have money?" She stares down at me like I'm just a kid looking for a freebie.

I run the numbers in my head. Converted to U.S. currency, it's about twenty-eight dollars. Between Madam Isis and Faisal, I won't have any money left. But how can I pass up a chance to speak with my dad?

"Five dinars," I say and then add *khamza* to let her know she's dealing with a pro. I also check to make sure Gordy is watching. He could stand to pick up a thing or two. I learned from the best, my Mom. She can out-bargain any shopkeeper. I notice Faisal gawking at me.

"Ashra," the fortuneteller says.

It's not one of the Arabic words I know, so I stare at her, copying what Mom does.

"Khamza, khalas." She throws up her palms. "Fifteen minutes." She motions to a table for two covered with a cloth.

Madam Isis settles on one stool and invites me to take the other. Gordy positions himself next to me while Faisal flattens himself into a rug covering the wall near the door.

Before I can ask about Dad, Madam Isis grabs my right hand and pulls it to her. She runs her fingers along my palm and gazes into my eyes. Her hands feel like ice against my sweaty palms.

"We're in a hurry." Gordy looks back at the door, still holding his nose.

"I know why you've come," Madam Isis says in a misty voice, drawing out the vowels of otherwise perfect English. "You seek what you have lost."

She really can read minds. I start to open my mouth, but Madam Isis's eyes, blackened by kohl powder, stop me. Stroking my palm, her fingers trace lines arching around the pad of my thumb. She closes her eyes and breathes deeply. "You, daughter of Huldu, Queen of the Nabateans, at last you have come home."

Gordy stifles a loud snort.

"Beware! Do not anger the spirits by speaking." Madam Isis parts her eyelids and gives Gordy a withering look. I clamp my teeth together to keep a giggle from escaping. Everyone in this market place has a shtick. It's how they talk the tourists into parting with their money. I still want to know what she has to say.

Madam Isis resumes her study of my palm, dirt and all. When the silence becomes as suffocating as the incense, she starts again.

"It is written you must seek the lost treasures of Petra, the jewels of the Queen of the Nabateans, daughter of Huldu."

Jewels? Now we're talking.

"Queen Huldu was the most beautiful woman of the land. A beauty like you, my little friend. People would travel days for a glimpse of her, with her black tresses and moonlit eyes. Few could resist her charms."

This is so worth every dinar.

"Queen Huldu lived in a tented palace in Petra." The fortuneteller paints the picture with her finger as she speaks, drawing me in.

"But not everyone admired her. There were the jealous ones too, none more envious than her cousin, Salome, who hated her for winning the King's heart. The Kingdom was very rich and powerful, you see. The Nabateans controlled the desert roads to the east, where they traded for frankincense and myrrh. My young friends, you have heard of frankincense and myrrh?"

I shake my head and beg her to explain.

"As precious as gold in the time of our forefathers, they were the incense and perfume of royalty."

The fortuneteller smiles and lowers her voice.

"This cousin Salome lived in the neighboring kingdom of Judea, in the Royal Court of King Herod. The Nabateans and the Judeans were enemies. Huldu, also a Judean, had been married to the King of the Nabateans to seal a peace treaty between the two peoples. Angered that Huldu was chosen instead of her, Salome began to plot with her servants and guards. She planned to kill Huldu, steal her jewels and her kingdom."

Madam Isis pauses. I lean in closer to encourage her to go on. I am certain this Salome girl would be no match for Queen Huldu.

"The Queen's spies told her of the plot as Princess Salome crossed the desert to the royal city of Petra. Queen Huldu decided to greet her cousin with a reception worthy of an emissary from the Kingdom of Judea. She could not harm Salome, at the risk of starting a new war between their people. She had to win her over with flattery and charm. As a precaution, Queen Huldu hid her jewels and the famed Golden Girdle, somewhere outside the Royal Enclave."

Now I know I have come to the right place.

"She did not reveal the location to anyone. Then, she mounted a white stallion, and with the King beside her, she rode through the mountain pass to meet her cousin. But tragedy struck. Her horse, frightened by a scorpion, threw her."

Madam Isis pinches my arm, mimicking a scorpion bite.

"She died in the arms of her beloved before Salome's arrival. The jewels were lost forever."

I realize I am holding my breath, terrified the scorpion is real.

"So the Golden Girdle's not a legend. It's for real?" Gordy gives me a sideways glance.

"Indeed. For thousands of years explorers and archaeologists have searched for it, convinced it remains hidden somewhere in

Petra. But a word of warning, death comes to those who enter Petra to steal its treasures." The pupils of her eyes dilate as if death excites her. "'Uzza protects her women. Beware of her curse." Madam Isis traces a shape on my hand before folding my fingers into my palm. It is the eye of 'Uzza.

"My payment, now."

It's like she slammed closed the book without letting me read the final chapter.

"But we still have five minutes," Gordy says.

"That is all. You must seek elsewhere." Madam Isis stands and waves her hand toward the door.

I don't want to leave. I still have so many questions. Is 'Uzza's eye a clue or a curse? Does Mom know this stuff? Is this is my one chance to ask about something else? About Dad? But Madam Isis just stands there, her arms crossed, eyes closed, like she is intending to blend back into the wall.

"You say you can contact the dead."

I hear a gasp. Faisal is at my side, wrenching me off the stool. "Ana, we go now. Yes?"

"Whom do you wish to speak with?"

"My dad." My voice cracks. "Jack Steppe."

The mistiness evaporates from Madam Isis's eyes when she repeats Dad's name.

Faisal drops my arm and scurries backwards so fast he thuds against the carpeted wall. Madam Isis remains still, except now her eyes stay open a slit, moving between Faisal and me.

"It would depend if the spirit is nearby and willing to talk."

"Please?" I take the money out of my backpack, my agreed payment of five dinars with a few extra coins to tempt the spirits.

Madam Isis walks to a corner table. She lights a flame in an oil lamp shaped like the genie ones in the Disney movies. The smell of sandalwood wafts toward me. She picks up a silver coffee pot with an extended spout and pours a black liquid into a tiny cup. Holding the delicate handle between her thumb and forefinger, she tips her head back and drinks the liquid with lightning speed, then snaps the cup upside down on a waiting saucer.

With saucer and oil lamp in hand, she glides back to the table and places them before me. She sits, both hands folded in front of her, eyes closed. She chants. I shut my eyes too. Her words and the sandalwood waft around me, under my nose, into my head, mixing with images of my dad, his voice, his laugh. I feel warm and tingly and strain my ears to hear his voice. And then a rush of air moves through the room. A wick smolders. Charms bang. The table lurches. Glass shatters. I open my eyes in time to see Faisal disappearing through the draped fabric hiding the exit. Madam Isis is standing, eyes burning holes through the draped door. Gordy is crouched, fists cocked, ready to protect me from...from...what? Djinn?

The coffee cup and saucer are on the floor in pieces.

"It's no good. The spirit will not reveal himself with these disturbances. Come back tomorrow, with more money."

KIBBEH BALLS AND MISTAKEN IDENTITY

We don't get far in our search for Faisal.

"Found you." Mrs. Brown grabs me in a vice-like grip. Gordy's held captive by her other hand. Mom's right about bad things happening in threes.

"We still have time for a quick lunch before the Deputy Minister of Antiquities himself gives us a tour of Petra." She steers both of us into a nearby cafe. I recognize her "don't-mess-with-me" face under her oversized brim. No longer a fugitive, I'm a hostage in Haddad's House of Hummus.

Mrs. Brown sniffs at my clothes for the second time today. "What is that smell?" She points to the back of the café at a battered door with "WC" hand lettered on it. I clutch my backpack trying to contain the putrid smell of Mom's secret. Both Gordy and I turn for the bathroom at the same time.

"Ana, leave your backpack. Gordon, come here."

Gordon? Mrs. Brown must be sore that we gave her the slip. I feel bad because by the sound of it, she's going to take it out on Gordy. I grip my backpack tighter and keep moving.

The bathroom has one door, no window and makes the inside of my backpack smell sweet by comparison. With escape not an option, I stand near the door, trying not to breathe, and think about Mr. Hasan. He said he's the Deputy Minister. Why is he taking us on a tour? If they've talked, he must have told Mrs. Brown about the fax. What happened to eviction-by-helicopter? Why an offer to take us on a tour if he wants to get rid of us? A sharp knock at the door startles me, and I inhale. Blech. I turn on the squeaky tap at the sink and wait until the brown colored water runs clear before sticking my hands into it. I unlock the door with my elbows and exit, my hands in the air, shaking them hard to dry faster.

Gordy stops talking as soon as he sees me and lowers his eyes to the playing cards on the table. He shuffles the deck, but the grin looks gone forever. Even worse, Faisal is still missing. Tomb Robber and Madam Isis have given me my first real clues to the Golden Girdle. How can I follow them if I'm trapped with Mrs. Brown?

"I thought we were going to have to send out a search party," Mrs. Brown says as I slide into my chair. The sunglasses are off, but the large hat remains in place. An elderly man piles plates of food in front of us. Did Mrs. Brown select all of this, and if so, how did she know what I liked or even how to order? I know from experience that ordering food in Arabic is hard. I once got goat eye soup when I thought I'd ordered a falafel.

I grab the nearest dish, which is full of olives and pickles, scoop them up with a triangle of pita and cram them in my mouth. I say a silent prayer to the food gods. We can't talk if our mouths are full. Mrs. Brown's rule, not mine.

Gordy reaches into a bowl in front of him.

"Don't use your fingers," Mrs. Brown says.

Gordy looks around. "There aren't any forks or spoons."

I hold up a wedge of pita bread and, using it like a spoon, dig into the bowl of hummus.

"Is that paper-mâché?" Gordy points at the hummus.

"Just try it," I say with my mouth full. Eating's making me feel hopeful.

Gordy picks up one piece of pita with two fingers and sticks it in the hummus.

"Use your other hand, Gordon," Mrs. Brown says, her lips pinched.

Without arguing, Gordy switches the bread to his right hand. His ears are bright pink. How did Mrs. Brown know?

"You can't eat with your left hand," I say.

"Why not?" Gordy shoves the pita and hummus in his mouth.

"It's custom. In the old days the Bedouin didn't have toilet paper, so they used their left hand to wipe their butts and the right hand for eating. Good system, huh?"

Gordy laughs so hard the pita and hummus spews back out. Mrs. Brown glares at me and calls the waiter to bring more napkins.

I pick up a kibbeh in a wedge of pita and shove it toward Gordy. "Try this, it's my favorite." Kibbeh is what I remember best from my last visit to Jerusalem. They have them in New York, but they don't taste half as good.

"What's in it?" Gordy breaks one in half and inspects the ground up meat mixed with pine nuts.

"Mystery meat, just try it."

"I was thinking...they don't eat weird things like cats or monkeys? Right? Or eyeballs. They don't eat eyeballs do they?"

I'm about to gross him out with a story about cow brains and spiny sea anemones, when a man in a white jalabiya appears at our table.

"Madam, I thought I recognized your voice. What an honor to see you here again."

I drop my napkin and dive under the table. It's the shopkeeper from Sinbad Souvenirs. The one whose store I destroyed. I'm sure I'm in trouble now. Will he make me pay? Or go back and spend the rest of my vacation cleaning up?

"I'm sorry, you must be mistaken," Mrs. Brown, says. "I don't know you."

I peer over the edge of the table. Mrs. Brown's lips are pinched into a tight frown. The hat hides the rest of her face.

"Aren't you—?"

"I'm sure we Americans must all sound alike. This is my first visit."

"Pardon me, Madam." The shopkeeper bows low while keeping his probing eyes on Mrs. Brown who is now signaling to the waiter.

"No bothering the customers." The old man who brought our food shoos the shopkeeper away. Mrs. Brown does not say anything, but I see a triangle patch of red appear on her chest. Kind of like Gordy's ears when he's nervous. I pull myself up into my chair, also relieved the man is gone.

"Finish up. We have a tour we don't want to miss." Mrs. Brown places her napkin over her uneaten food and signals to the waiter.

"Have you been here before?" I guard my plate from her outstretched hand.

"I just said I had not," Mrs. Brown says, with an edge on the T's of just and not.

"You ordered all my favorites and know the customs."

Mrs. Brown laughs. The first time I have seen her teeth this entire trip. "I asked the waiter to bring the house specialties. As for local manners, I took the time to study. Have you?"

"What?"

"Your manners. You seem to have a habit of running off and diving under tables. Would your mother approve of that behavior?"

"You're not my mother."

Mrs. Brown sighs. "I know you'd rather not be here with me, but I'm doing my best to look after you. I could use some cooperation. Gordy told me you went to a fortuneteller who told you a tale about the Golden Girdle, and you asked about your father. I can't help but think this is what's upsetting you."

My suspicions switch from Mrs. Brown to Gordy as my eyes jump from mother to son. I can't believe it. He told her about the fortuneteller and the Golden Girdle? He's blabbered all of it to Mrs. Brown. The rat. I wished I hadn't shared my kibbeh.

THE SEVENTH WONDER
AND A GRINNING CAMEL

Mrs. Brown introduces us to Mr. Hasan as we bake in the sun outside the gates to Petra's archeological park. I have lost my sunglasses, again, and have to squint my eyes just to see. Mr. Hasan's still sweating in his shiny suit, but now he's added a white Panama hat. He looks like a gangster from the old black-and-white movies. When he greets me, it's like he doesn't know me. He doesn't mention the helicopter or going home, but gives me one of those fake adult smiles and tells me how much he's enjoyed working with my mom. Even weirder, he keeps complimenting Mrs. Brown, saying stupid things about how nice it is she's here, and he hopes everything is to her liking. Either he's embarrassed he tried to get rid of me, or Mrs. Brown makes him nervous. Or maybe, he's the imposter Mom warned me about.

"It's a shame Dr. Steppe can't join us, but we're so lucky to have such an important government official giving us a private tour," Mrs. Brown says.

Mrs. Brown's tight lips give me the feeling she doesn't mean any of it.

A boy with a cardboard sign tugs at my sleeve and pantomimes taking a picture. His price is half a dinar. I find my camera in the outer pocket of my backpack and hand it to him, figuring I can add it to my growing scrapbook of photos taken all over the world. The click of the camera sends Mrs. Brown to the boy's side, demanding to see the picture.

Maybe I'm imagining things, but I swear Mrs. Brown flicks out the memory chip before dropping my camera in her large bag.

"Hey," I say. "That's mine."

"Honey, it looks expensive. Why don't I hold it for you, and you can tell me when you want to take another picture."

"But it's my camera."

Mrs. Brown doesn't answer. Instead she starts talking to Mr. Hasan as they head into the narrow opening of the rocks.

I run in front of her and block the way. Saved to that memory chip are pictures of Mom and Dad from our trip to Egypt a year ago. There's a special one with the Great Pyramid in the background. Dad has Mom and me in each arm, hugging us hard. I'm laughing because I think my eyes are going to pop out.

Mom is either sneaking a kiss or whispering something in his ear. She looks happy. Dad has on his just-wait-there's-more grin. It was the best trip ever.

"Give me my camera," I demand.

Mrs. Brown stops. "Is that how you talk to adults? We can go back to the hotel." Mr. Hasan has his red handkerchief out again.

I bite my lip and look to Gordy. He's shaking his head.

"May I have my camera, please?" I emphasize *my*, not the please, between clenched teeth.

Mrs. Brown reaches into her bag. "Don't complain to me when you lose it. And put your backpack on with both straps. You don't want someone to snatch it, do you?"

I grumble that I can wear my backpack anyway I like. I never use both straps. I press open the back of the camera to check for the chip when Gordy moves to my side. He whispers a warning not to cause a scene, promising to get it back later.

"Whose side are you on?" I shoot back.

Gordy looks down, his bangs falling across his eyes, voice still a whisper. "Mother doesn't like her picture taken. I was thinking if you ever want to see the chip again, you better let me take care of it."

I take off at a run, leaving Mrs. Brown to eat my dust. If I find she's stolen from me, she'll be the one begging and saying please. Where ever we are going I will be first, and I want to make sure she keeps her grubby paws off of my backpack.

I can't stay angry with Mrs. Brown, not because she doesn't deserve it, but because of Nabatean magic. Not the hocus-pocus kind, but the awe-inspiring, I-can't-believe-my-eyes kind.

I walk through a narrow gorge called the Siq, trapped on both sides by claustrophobic cliffs of red and pink rock. The sign at the entrance said only welcomed guests were allowed to pass. The Nabateans pummeled their enemies to death by rocks thrown from the cliffs.

I, the long lost daughter of Queen Huldu, am not pelted by stones as I stroll through the gorge, but am welcomed by subjects offering me gifts—local boys trying to sell me stuff. The cliffs twist and turn, shading us one minute then letting the sun hit us like a blast furnace the next. In places the gorge closes in. I stretch my arms out and touch both walls at once. I understand why it was impossible for an army to sneak into Petra, even if they could find the hidden entrance. I glance back and notice Gordy guzzling from his water bottle. I am drenched with sweat and wish I were floating in the hotel pool about now.

The Siq boxes us in tighter, cutting us off from the world and sky. I feel like I'm being squeezed into an ant hole. And then I see it. A slit of light. For a moment Gordy and I stand elbow to elbow in shock. Through the crack in the rock, I spot the beginnings of a reddish-gold building, carved out of the mountain, and taller than the trees in Central Park. At the top of the building is an urn, like a supersized offering to the gods. A real live, stinky camel rests at the foot of the building, its long legs folded under its body, looking like a toy against this backdrop. A Bedouin in a jalabiya with a red-and-white checkered kiffiyah on his head walks in and out of my view.

"Hurry," I say. We have to slide through the opening before this magic kingdom disappears.

Once through the crack, light floods the area around us. We stand before the building carved out of the rock and rising as high as the red cliffs. The glow of the afternoon sun tinges the rocks with a golden shimmer, making them look like they're on fire.

"The Treasury," Mr. Hasan says coming up behind me. He doesn't act like he's in the presence of the most amazing Wonder of the Ancient World. I am rooted there with Gordy, my mouth open.

"Is that where Queen Huldu kept her treasure?" I manage to say. I'm thinking a treasury could be the perfect place to hide the Golden Girdle.

Mr. Hasan stops for a moment and looks toward Mrs. Brown before answering me.

"It is an empty tomb. Others like you believed it might contain hidden riches. See the bullet holes in the stone? They are from the rifles of treasure hunters seeking hidden chambers."

"Then why do they call it the Treasury and not the Tomb?"

Mr. Hasan takes off his hat and sweeps it toward the mountains. "These are all tombs. Hundreds of them. The Nabateans lived in tents like the Bedu today, but they were trader kings. Their camels were ships and the vast desert, their sea. You see the Nabateans knew the secret routes of the desert. For a thousand years, they transported riches across this sea. The journeys were hard. Many died from lack of water or food, or bandits. In ancient times, they dominated the markets. The heart of the Nabatean kingdom was here, in the city of Petra, a fortress within the rocks, rich beyond all imagination."

A light breeze kicks up sand and dirt; thousands of years of dust plaster the surfaces of the building and me. I glance up at the ledge with a giant urn carved out of the rock and see a Bedouin sitting high above us, like on a throne in the sky. There is no railing, or anything to keep him from sliding off the rock in the next gust of wind. I look again and recognize Faisal. He's here, watching us. Hope surges through my body. If bad things happen in threes, maybe so do good things. Faisal must be back because he has ideas on where to find the Golden Girdle, and not just because I owe him money.

I want to tell Gordy about Faisal, but Mrs. Brown's watching me.

The clomping of a donkey sounds behind me. I step aside to give it as much room as it wants. I recognize the white suit of the rider: Tomb Robber from the souq. He sees me too, and, for an instant, our eyes lock. The dislike is mutual. I bet he's figured out I took his envelope. I'm not afraid. I'm going to tell Mom about him as soon as I find her.

He gives his donkey a kick, like he intends to run me over. I duck behind Mrs. Brown. But the donkey has other ideas. It's nibbling on the straw hat of an unsuspecting tourist. I wonder why Tomb Robber's here so late in the day. Maybe he has an appointment with one of the archeologists. Or maybe it's easier to steal in the dark after all the tourists are gone.

As we leave the Treasury, locals fight for the chance to guide us. Mr. Hasan waves them away with a flick of his wrist. We pass corrals filled with donkeys for hire. I flick my wrist and shake my head no to the hawkers, just like Mr. Hasan. Donkeys, like camels, stink, and one bit me during that visit to the pyramids in Egypt. I'm not riding on a donkey. I'll walk until my blisters get blisters before I'll ride a donkey. The sellers don't take no for an answer so I settle for a cloth hat—no straw for me—with a floppy brim that hides my entire face. I buy Gordy a cap decorated with a grinning camel even though Mrs. Brown tries to talk me out of it.

"Thanks," Gordy says. "I should be buying you something, since you're paying for Faisal, but I don't have any money..."

I groan. Gordy doesn't have a clue when to keep his trap shut.

"…I was thinking every time I wear this, I'd remember this first trip."

"First trip? There's more planned?" Does he know something I don't? Gordy I could get used to, but not Mrs. Brown. Never.

"First trip ever." Gordy grins, pulling on his new cap. "Outside of New York, I mean."

I relax. That explains a lot. I don't tell him how silly he looks, especially when it forces his bangs even lower over his eyes.

Mr. Hasan has removed his suit jacket and continues to lead us past a theater with stone steps as seats, down a path lined by a row of fat columns, all broken off at different heights. "Wadi al-Mahtuh," he says. "Wadi is a dry riverbed. Hundreds of thousands of years ago, the river cut through the rocks and made the canyon. With the river gone, the Nabateans built their city here in the protection of the mountain walls. As you can see, little is left of the city itself. This is called Colonnade Street."

Maybe it was once a street, but I feel like I'm standing in a bowling alley for giants, the mountains on either side framing the path, the columns as the pins. One mega bowling ball tumbling down the canyon would wipe out everything, the columns, the theatre, the half building with the sculptures of winged lions and me. There's no place to run and hide.

"Where'd the river go?" Gordy says, the grinning camel bouncing up and down.

"Desertification has changed the climate here, making it more arid over the centuries. During our winter season, a small stream will form from runoff of what little rain falls on the Petra Mountains." Mr. Hasan points to a reddish-black patch of dirt snaking along the canyon floor. "Twice in my lifetime the runoff created a raging river, and we had to close the archaeological park. Today, and most of the year, the riverbed is dry."

Mom once told me about a British diplomat and his wife driving across a desert in the southern part of Morocco who didn't pay attention to the rain falling in the mountains just north of them. They drowned in the flats of the Sahara desert; their bodies washed up twenty-five kilometers away. I wonder who could be dense enough not to notice when it starts raining in a desert. I look around again. It's summer now so I'm not worried at all about a sudden flood. We could be on the moon. The canyon is littered with boulders, big and small. Everything is the same color, brown with tints of red and yellow. Even the few olive trees blend in.

"Observe those cuts in the rock wall up there." Mr. Hasan points up into the towering mountain. "Those channels collect rainwater and send it into deep cisterns cut into the rocks. Those wells provided water year around. Where there was water, civilization thrived."

"So the Nabateans got rich off the water?" Gordy asks. "I thought they had treasures of gold and silver?" Gordy gives me his quick grin.

"I'd like a swim in one of those cisterns right now. I'd even pay," I shoot back.

"Water was far too precious to waste on bathing. The Nabateans, like the Bedu today, take sand baths. Water is used only for ritual bathing before prayer."

Sand baths? I check for a wink or a smile, but Mr. Hasan doesn't act like he made a joke as he pats the sweat under his chin with his red handkerchief. If it's true, it could explain why Faisal looks so dusty.

"As for gold and silver," Mr. Hasan continues, "the Nabatean markets were filled with crowds and goods from all over. Traders brought silk from the Orient. Lapis lazuli from Afghanistan. Frankincense and myrrh were the most precious. The Nabatean traders knew where to find these great treasures in the Arabian Desert, and only they could survive the journey. Many others tried and failed."

Mr. Hasan reminds me a lot of Mom; he enjoys explaining the building and irrigation systems designed by the Nabateans. The more he talks, the more I question my suspicions. This man is seriously into ancient history. He cares a lot more about long-lost civilizations than about the present, just like Mom.

The hot afternoon air presses in on me, making it hard to keep clear thoughts in my head. Mr. Hasan leads us up out of the wadi and through the jagged boulders. He tells us how a massive earthquake destroyed the city. Without water, the people moved away and over time, the stone city disappeared under the sand– and from people's memory. The steps are uneven, and my footing slips on the shifting rocks. I feel like the ground is wiggling under me, and I will disappear under the sand as well.

Gordy charges ahead with Mr. Hasan. I follow with Mrs. Brown. Gordy's chatting away like he could climb and talk all day. Sweat stains the back of Mr. Hasan's gray shirt. I wonder what they are talking about. I hope Gordy doesn't blab to Mr. Hasan about our treasure hunt. It won't keep Mr. Hasan from sending me back to New York. I feel a knot in my stomach. Will Mr. Hasan tell Gordy about the fax and Mom not wanting to see me? As much as I try to believe otherwise, her fax was clear: *Change of plans. Don't come.* I try to swallow the memory away, but my mouth has no spit.

"Are you feeling okay, Ana?" Mrs. Brown steadies me as I stumble on loose rocks.

"Just hot," I say quickly.

"Here, drink some water." Mrs. Brown hands me a bottle of cold water.

I guzzle half of it and then stop. "Sorry, there's still some left."

"I bought it for you. You look upset. What's wrong, honey?"

I drink another mouthful of water and splash some on my face to cover up the tears. "Mom," I say.

Mrs. Brown puts her arm around me, her hand on the strap of my backpack. "I know it's hard to understand your mother's priorities right now."

I nod. Sometimes Mrs. Brown can be nice.

"Gordy says you two are on a treasure hunt. I think he was teasing me, saying it was a real treasure. Something about a golden girdle and that you have some clues?"

"What?" My head snaps up, and I turn to face at her.

"Maybe I can help. If finding a treasure would cheer you up."

The knot in my stomach grows tighter. I pull away and climb the steps faster. It's my adventure, not hers.

Mrs. Brown keeps pace, smiling. I see two perfect rows of white teeth.

"Did your mother leave you a clue?"

"No!" I don't look at Mrs. Brown, but continue to move in front of her. Gripping the strap of my backpack, I wonder if Mrs. Brown, like Mom, has a built-in lie detector. Mom always knows when I am lying. Dad used to tell me only a pro can beat the Mom-detector, and I should stick to the truth. Once I asked him if he was a pro. He looked shocked, and he scolded me, saying dissembling should be reserved for exceptional situations, like saving lives, not covering up misdeeds. Dad never used the word lying.

I'm relieved when I reach a modern building. The Petra Museum. Cold air is blasting out the entryway, like the open door to a freezer. The radio attached to Mr. Hasan's belt starts crackling. He doesn't even say good-bye, just turns and takes the stairs by twos. I hear something about a scorpion and a tourist until he is too far away to hear any more.

I shudder. Scorpion bites don't kill you at once. It takes a couple of hours for the poison to pulse through to your heart or lungs. You can feel your body dying beat by beat as the poison paralyzes you, your tongue swells up, and you can't stop drooling. During our trip to Egypt, I saw a dog dying from a scorpion sting. I hope Petra has a hospital.

"You have an hour in the museum, and then we need to head back to the hotel," Mrs. Brown says, coming up behind me.

I jump when she touches my shoulder, feeling stupid at once for my overactive imagination. Mrs. Brown isn't going to sting me. She's just nosy. But I wonder if Mr. Hasan's helicopter is waiting for us, and if that's why we have to go back to the hotel. Mr. Hasan has something up his sleeve. I can feel it. Just because he's the deputy minister of antiquities and an archaeologist doesn't mean he's a good guy. I'm keeping my eye on him until I find Mom.

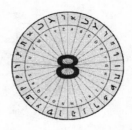

Two Heads and Twelve Signs

The Petra Museum is crammed full of bits of stuff: broken pottery, parts and pieces of sculpture, and reconstructed jewelry. Most people would throw these things in the trash, but archeologists dust them off and put them behind glass.

I study the museum brochure with a drawing of the floor plan and wonder how I'm going to kill an hour in this place. There's a main room with five smaller rooms forming a semicircle around it. At least the thermostat is set to brain chill. I glance over at Mrs. Brown. She looks bored already and is flipping through one of the museum brochures, while staring out the window. It's like she's trying to get someone's attention on the other side of the glass. I want to sneak a look, but a distracted Mrs. Brown means a chance to ditch her.

I pull Gordy into the first open door hoping to find someone who looks like an archaeologist to ask about Mom.

Gordy doesn't make it past the first life-sized glass case. He stops and stares, transfixed by a two-headed monster. The sign at the monster's feet reads "Ancestor Statue, Ain Ghazal; 7000-6000 BCE." The sculpture is a blotchy plaster blob with two heads. Each head has large eyes outlined in black, with a carved out nose and mouth, looking more like a space alien than anyone's grandpa. It has no arms, and one big block for legs. I step closer and gaze from head to head.

"It looks like us." Gordy hops behind me and sticks his head out over my left shoulder. "Greetings Ancestor!" Gordy calls out.

I see our two-headed reflection in the glass. We look totally weird, but it's just like this trip. One thing's for certain; if I'm going to be stuck with Gordy, it will be my head we follow.

I notice Tomb Robber out of the corner of my eye. He heads into the next room. I give Gordy a sharp elbow and jerk my head to follow. We slip into the room and hide behind a life-sized photo of a female statue.

Tomb Robber stops in front a case along the back wall. He drops down on his haunches and pulls a penknife from his pocket. He runs the blade between the clear top and the base of the case. He places his hands on the sides and rocks it a few times. Satisfied, he stands again, hands on the glass, but yanks his hands away when three tourists talking loudly in French enter the room. He leaves without spotting either Gordy or me.

"He was trying to steal something. Where's security?" I say. I've spent my life in museums where just breathing hard can set off the alarm system. I've had personal experience.

The tourists move on, and Gordy and I make a beeline for the case. A gold disk, the size of a hockey puck, glows in the soft lighting. It looks like what I saw Tomb Robber show the shopkeeper at Sinbad Souvenirs. So the shopkeeper was right; it's not one of a kind. Maybe it is like those collections of small stuffed animals, where if you collect them all you win a prize.

"It's a crab," Gordy whispers.

The gold disk is embossed with the outline of a crab with two big pincher claws. The shopkeeper said Tomb Robber's was a lion. I lean down for a closer look but stop when more tourists enter the gallery, in case someone accuses me of messing with the case. I tell Gordy we should leave, but he won't take his eyes off the crab. I cross to the opposite side of the room near the oversized photo and act casual. At first the statue reminds me of a woman holding the world on her shoulders, but I change my mind after staring a bit longer and reading the sign.

Nike and the Nabatean Zodiac. I remember the picture Mom ripped out from some catalog. It's the same statue.

I move in for a closer look. In the center of the stone disk is a carving of a lady wearing a crown; "Tyche, the Goddess of Fortune," the display says. Animals are carved around Tyche. Nike isn't carrying the world; she's hefting a zodiac calendar, with each animal representing a different lunar month. I see a carved crab and lion, but this zodiac doesn't look anything like what I'm used to. I can't find a goat for December, my birth month.

"There's something weird about this," I tell Gordy when he joins me.

"What?" Gordy's not paying attention but is looking over at another large wall display.

"All the great constellations live very long since stars can't alter physics."

"Huh?" Gordy turns and frowns at me like I've gone nuts.

"It's a mnemonic, a way to remember the order of the zodiac. *All* stands for Aries, the ram, and it should be at the top. *Stars* means Sagittarius, and it should be on the left side of the circle." I point to the eight o'clock spot on the circle. "The lion is in the centaur's place. That's not right."

Gordy cocks his head to the right. "Aries doesn't look like a ram either, just an ugly lady. Maybe the carver messed up. Maybe the stars were in different places back then."

"You're the one who's messed up. Stars don't—" Gordy interrupts me before I tell him stars are not like a deck of cards to be shuffled about in the sky.

"Something else is missing," Gordy says

"What?"

70

"This family tree of Nabatean royalty is all wrong." He points to the wall display listing the kings and queens of the Nabateans.

My eyes narrow on the genealogical chart, trying to figure out what's not there. "How d' you know?"

"I was thinking I don't see Anatolia Steppe, great, great, great, great, great, granddaughter of Queen Huldu." A grin sneaks across his face.

"That's Ana Steppe to you." I give him a smirk back and then study the chart. Queen Huldu's name is printed next to King Aretas. It's proof Madam Isis wasn't making it up. My heart skips in my chest. "It's not like I'm in line for the throne, but Queen Huldu once lived here, and that means we're one step closer to finding the Golden Girdle."

"I was thinking all we need now is a treasure map," Gordy says. "And...and..."

"What?" I ask turning to see what Gordy is staring at.

Tomb Robber is eyeball to eyeball with Gordy and me. His white shirt's no longer quite so white. He grabs Gordy by the collar. "What are you little pickpockets up to now? Something for your thieving mother or whatever you call her?"

I look around for Mrs. Brown and tell myself not to panic. Dad always said the best defense is offense. "Are you calling me a crook?" I flare my nostrils for the full effect.

71

He cocks his head, shifting his attention from Gordy to me. He reminds me of Principal Frost peering over the top of her spectacles. "She thinks she can hide behind little fingers, does she? Brilliant. Except I'm on to you."

I just stare and wonder if he knows we saw him messing with the case.

"You've been warned."

Before I zing back a clever response, he pushes Gordy away and disappears into the next room.

"He must not know he's talking to royalty." Gordy straightens his shirt.

We both snicker. But Gordy's ears are bright red. He was scared too.

Gordy fingers the small pocket of his backpack. "What do you think he'll do if we find the clues first?"

"He can threaten us all he wants. But I'm not giving up the hunt."

"What about Mr. Hasan?"

"What do you mean?" I ask.

"Mr. Hasan asked me if you knew anything about the treasure, because if you did, you needed his protection. He said dangerous people are after the Golden Girdle, and they would bury anyone to get to it first."

Dangerous people? Like Tomb Robber? Or like Mr. Hasan? A chill rips though me.

"What'd you say?"

"I asked him what a girdle was."

I roll my eyes, wondering how anyone can be so ignorant.

"If I'm going to help you hunt for a treasure, I was thinking I should know what it looks like. Maybe how big it is. How much it weighs—"

"A girdle's a special kind of underwear women wear to squeeze their fat rolls in, so they look skinny. Kind of like super tight bike shorts."

"We're searching for underwear?"

"Golden underwear. I'm pretty sure it has jewels on it."

"Jewels? That doesn't sound comfortable."

I decide we need to see an example to solve this mystery. The only clothing is on the mannequins in the next room. We circle around to the backside of the female mannequin. She's wearing a black robe covered with embroidery so the dress appears more red and gold than black. She's topped off with a crown and a fancy necklace with a pendant that reminds me of the Tomb Robber's drawing of 'Uzza's eye. I figure she's supposed to be one of the queens. I kneel down and slip my hand under the hem of the dress, but Gordy stops me.

"What are you doing?"

"Showing you what ancient girdles look like."

"I can't. That's a…she's a… private girl stuff!"

"It's just a big doll." I whip the dress up to knee level, but it's heavy, and the mannequin starts to tilt forward, away from me. I tug to keep it from falling even as Her Majesty slips away.

"Help me," I whisper.

Gordy attempts to block the fall as the mannequin hits the floor. There is a sound of ripping as I scramble away and ram into Gordy. We both take down the male mannequin. Next thing I know, I'm gazing up through a pile of arms and legs at the woman in a green headscarf with a nametag that identifies her as the assistant curator and the double-wide cop who looks a lot like the cop from the souq. A badge on his chest says Royal Antiquities Police. First I panic, then I begin making excuses a mile a minute. Gordy spills the beans. Right then and there, he tells them we wanted to see a golden girdle. Did the underwear come with jewels or just plain gold? I'm expecting the handcuffs to be locked on any second. We'll face charges of attempted looting and destroying plastic property. Instead the woman starts laughing.

Laughing.

My face grows red hot. I don't get the joke.

The woman in the green scarf reaches out and helps us up from the pile, scolding us for not following the rules. She points to a boldly printed sign in five different languages—four of them I can read—instructing no touching. When I tap her forearm with an extra plastic hand, she takes it, shaking the finger at me. I figure now is not the right time to ask if she knows Mom.

"It's not funny. It was an accident."

She bursts into laughter again. "A girdle is a ceremonial belt. Not a lady's undergarment."

I mumble we knew that but thought it was hidden under the robe. I don't look at Gordy, but I can feel his eyes on me. I'm pretty sure he's thinking I don't know what I'm doing. I'm thinking about Dad's Rule number 3: assume nothing.

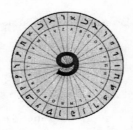

Ancient Alphabets
and Modern Thieves

Gordy and I escape to the next room. I have my hands deep in my jean pockets, hoping the double-wide policeman watching our backs will understand the international sign of no further touching. So far, this room seems pretty safe. Almost everything is locked behind glass. Wall-sized displays show ancient Nabatean writing systems. One of the displays is an interactive game showing how to transliterate the Nabatean letters. Gordy is in front of it in seconds while I move around the cases, pausing in front of each one, like I'm studying the items. I'm not. I'm using the reflection in the glass to watch the door. Sure enough, I see Double-Wide's image move across the glass. Clack. Clack. I hear the smacking of the worry beads. I cut through to the last of the small rooms, with Double-Wide following a few minutes later. Clack. Clack. Double-Wide flicks the beads double-hard. I look around for Mrs. Brown in case Double-Wide gets any ideas. Where is she when I need her?

I circle back to find Gordy. He's still playing the game, hitting the buttons real fast like he's flipping cards from his deck, not breaking the code of a long forgotten language.

"It's an educational tool, not a toy," I say, hoping there's safety in numbers...or alphabets.

"You should try this. The Nabatean alphabet is like ours. Each letter for a different sound. Except they have two different H's and three S's and, get this, no vowels. See this pi-looking thing, it's an H, like in happy. This soccer goal post thing is the KH sound, like you got a hairball..."

I can't concentrate on what Gordy is saying. My thoughts are on Double-Wide who's now standing in the doorway, watching us. Gordy keeps hitting buttons, and the man keeps staring. Dad always advised keeping adversaries off balance. I turn around and stick my tongue out. He scowls and then disappears from view.

"That's the same policeman from the souq." I take a victory march around Gordy.

Gordy grunts and continues playing his game.

"I'm following him."

Double-Wide heads down a narrow hall and a flight of stairs. He disappears behind a door marked "No Admittance, Museum Employees Only." I test the handle. It isn't locked. I push it open an inch, but can't see anything in the black void. I get this twangy feeling. Should I go in or not?

"Whatcha doing?"

My heart jumps.

It's Gordy.

"Don't sneak up on me," I say between clenched teeth.

"You're the one sneaking. Read the sign," Gordy says. "What if we get caught?"

"We won't, if you keep quiet." I raise a finger to my lips so Gordy understands there will be no debate or "thinking," as he calls it.

The door opens into a narrow passage way carved from rock. The floor is now dirt, no longer marble, and the lights are few. Once my eyes adjust to the darkness, I see stacks of crates along the walls, and an old sarcophagus, probably stuffed with a moldy old mummy. I shiver. This is the creepiest museum basement I've been in. That's when I hear voices. Men talking in Arabic, but I only catch a few words. Things like *careful* and *slowly*. We stand still as the sarcophagus and watch Double-Wide and another man huddle around a crate.

The stocky man, his face covered with a red-and-white kiffiyah, seems to be in charge. He points at a large dark stencil on top of the crate, marking it *Petra B132*. He hands Double-Wide an automatic drill and tells him to open the crate. One-by-one, Double-Wide removes eight screws, freeing the lid.

Red-and-White reaches into the crate and pulls out straw and then a dusty looking vase. Double-Wide brings over a tall basket, and the vase and straw are piled inside. Several more items are added to other baskets, topped with straw and then a layer of oranges and figs. They load the baskets into the back of the van pulled into a loading dock. When the van doors slam shut, I see a picture of fruits and vegetables painted on the back.

"They're stealing," I whisper.

"You should go get help."

Me? My legs are frozen in place. I push on them, but they won't move.

Gordy opens his mouth to say something more, but nothing comes out. His eyes go wide, like he's having trouble breathing.

Clack. Clack.

"She'll not be happy," Double-Wide says. "I save you for her."

My eyes fix on his hand crushed around the worry beads. Maybe following people into rooms marked off limits was not one of my best ideas, but it's not illegal. Then again, this isn't America. Who decides the rules in Petra? He said 'she'. She who? My mom? Before I can scream, Double-Wide grabs both Gordy and me in each of his hands. I kick and flail and try to bite, but I can't stop him from shoving us inside an empty crate.

The lid slams shut. Instant darkness. I hear the sound of an automatic drill, tightening two screws along the top.

Buried Treasure
and Slap Swears

I now know what it feels like to be buried alive. At first everything is quiet, eerily calm, except for my heart that sounds like a donkey cart running over cobblestones in the souq. And then I go crazy. I scream. I claw. I elbow. I kick. Somehow I've got to make the boards of the crate pop open. Nothing budges except Gordy beside me.

"You're squishing me," Gordy says.

Gordy pushes back, but being pinned down only makes me fight harder until I get tired. I wrap my braids around my neck and fold my arms over my chest, closing my eyes. I saw a picture in one of Mom's catalogs of a mummified body of a queen, and this was how she looked when they dug her up thousands of years later. If this is my fate, I might as well look like a queen.

I hear Gordy sniffing. Is he crying?

"What stinks?" Gordy whispers. "Did you have a, um, accident?"

"I did not," I say.

"Well, something smells bad."

"Yeah, being nailed into this coffin stinks."

"What do you think they'll do to us?" Gordy whispers.

I fight against the tears welling up in my eyes. Mom doesn't care I'm here, but Mrs. Brown will search for us. I take back all the bad thoughts I had about Mrs. Brown. She cares about me, and she knows we're here. Maybe not in this exact crate. But my stinky backpack will lead her here.

"Your mom will find us." I fight a growing feeling I can't breathe. I wonder how much air is in our crate. Ten minutes? Five? Gordy's small. Maybe he doesn't use much air.

"It'd be better if my mother isn't the one to find us."

"I don't think we should be picky." I start banging on the crate again. "HELP."

Silence. I'm assuming there's still air in the crate because if I were dead I wouldn't feel this scared. "Don't just lie there. Do something," I yell in Gordy's ear.

Gordy pulls away. His body slams against the far wall of the crate rocking it. I hear a soft "ouch," and then he says, "Do you bruise easily?"

"Whyyyyy?" Does he plan to pummel me for screaming? I hold my hands up to protect my face.

"I've been thinking. We might die if we stay here or we might die breaking out. Or someone could rescue us or we could rescue ourselves—"

"Or we could die debating the point."

"If we both roll at the same time, we can get this crate to fall off the one below it, and when it hits the concrete floor, it will split in two."

"What if we split in two?"

"What if Double-Wide comes back?" Gordy says.

"He said 'she' would be mad. Who do you think 'she' is?"

There is silence for once from Gordy.

"Well?"

"Let's roll this thing," Gordy says.

"On the count of three." As I count the numbers down, Gordy and I brace our bodies against the frame of the box and rock. The crate begins to tip and then settles back down. We rock again, and the crate shifts. On the third heave, the crate topples off the box below and slams over on its side on the concrete floor. My head smacks against the wood in the force of the fall. I see flashing white shapes. They are not from outside the crate, but in my aching head.

"Are you still alive?" Fingers press into me.

"No." I shift and get my feet back underneath me. We push and pull until both our heads point in the "this side is up" direction. I wiggle my entire body a few times just to make sure the cracking sound was one of the boards and not me. And then I feel around for the broken board. It's underneath me.

I groan. "We have to roll again."

Gordy grumbles. "Even if we get out of here alive, they know we saw them. That double-sized guy is probably already telling his boss about us. My mother is going to be so—"

"Knowing we're here and getting their mitts on us are two different things. I'm not making it easy for them."

We rock faster and faster. Gordy's like a human jackhammer. The crate flips over one half turn. Not perfect, but enough to free the side with the cracked board. "Kick as hard as you can."

It takes a few minutes, but we manage to kick the board free of the crate. I stick my arm out and try to wedge my head, but it won't fit. We're still trapped.

"At least we have fresh air," Gordy says.

Staring through the opening, I sigh. I don't know why I didn't see it before. Lying on the floor not far from the crate is the drill. Double-Wide must have left it on top of our crate after he sealed us in. It fell when the crate did.

"Stick your arms out and help me slide." We dog paddle inch by inch along the dirt floor as fast as we can. I stretch my arms and make contact with the drill. I slip it through the narrow opening and drill holes like my life depends on it—because it does. We kick another board free and wiggle out. Something hard rolls into me. I pick it up and find I'm holding the golden disk with the embossed crab.

"Where'd this come from?" I look around in case any other clues might fall from the sky.

"I might have taken it," Gordy says just above a whisper.

"What do you mean *might have*?"

Gordy doesn't say anything.

"That's stealing," I say. "If I'm a litterbug, you're a thief!"

Gordy snatches back the gold piece. "I'm protecting it. Tomb Robber wants it and was waiting for the museum to close to come back and get it."

"Okay...?" What I'm really thinking is Mom would have me on my hands and knees cleaning and dusting every inch of this museum if she caught me even touching it, let alone taking it out of the museum. But Mom's not here, and Gordy's right about not letting Tomb Robber get it. "We have to get out of this place before anyone finds us."

We find the loading dock empty, and the door locked shut. But set inside the larger door is a smaller one. My hand is on the knob. It wiggles. A way out?

I look down at the threshold. Once I step over it, I'm officially a thief too. What would Dad do? He'd remind me of Dad's Rule Number 4: keep your options open.

"We can't tell anyone we took this," I tell Gordy before opening the door. "Or that we're looking for the Golden Girdle.

No one will believe us about Tomb Robber, unless we have some proof. I mean no one. Your mom included."

Gordy has a look which makes me worry he's going to blow our cover.

"Slap swear, no tattling."

I reach out my hand, palm extended and firm. Gordy looks me in the eyes. He raises his hand.

"I swear to tell no one," he says solemnly.

"I swear to tell no one," I repeat. My right hand connects with his left cheek. Gordy's eyes widen, just for a second before his hand connects with my cheek. The sting of the slap seals the promise for both of us. Nothing can break a slap swear. It's an unbreakable oath.

A Djinn Block and
a Tall Mountain

The door lets us out on the backside of the museum and into the burning Petra air. We slide low along the rocky outcrop while I consider our next move. That's when I feel a hand on my shoulder and see a flash of red and white. I almost pee my pants thinking its Double-Wide's partner in crime.

"Miss Ana—"

"Faisal!" It comes out more like Iiiiisall!

"You must—"

"Why'd you run out on us?" I demand.

"No run."

"You left Madam Isis like the djinn were after you."

Faisal looks away, shifting his feet.

"Why?"

Faisal crouches down so we are eye to eye. I smell mint on his breath and wonder if that is the Arab version of garlic, meant to keep away the evil spirits. "Jack Steepp." The words are not even a whisper, just air.

I pull back in surprise. Why should my dad scare him?

"I guide Jack Steepp. He pay hundred dollars American for Faisal help."

"Whaaaaat?" I lose my balance and sit down hard on a rock.

"Faisal help Jack Steepp." Faisal doesn't look proud. He looks miserable, like he might run away again.

I grab his hand. "You saw my dad? When? Where?"

Faisal tries to free his hand, but I'm not letting go until I get answers.

"Five moons ago. Here."

"He was...alive?" I stammer.

Faisal nods.

Dad's alive! My skin tingles and my insides swell and want to burst. I knew he couldn't be dead. I love him too much for him to be gone forever. No wonder Madam Isis couldn't talk to him. He's not in the spirit world. He was here and then went somewhere. And that's why they wouldn't let me see Dad's body and there was only a memorial service, not a funeral. "Do you know where he went, what he did?" I have a thousand questions on my tongue.

"He asks too many questions. He walk into desert with bad men." Faisal peers over the rocks. He frowns. "You go now. Bad men look for kids. Go."

"But he is alive?"

"Ana, you go!"

"No! Answer me."

"Faisal knows men still look for him last week like he is with living."

I remember the day Dad left on his business trip. He said he'd bring me back a new journal from Europe. He didn't say anything about coming to Jordan. Mom didn't either. Faisal says five months ago. That's one month after the men in dark suits came to the house to talk to Mom. When they left, Mom didn't walk them to the door. She sat in front of the fireplace, crying. She wouldn't tell me anything except Dad died in an accident in Europe. Not Jordan. Not Petra. Europe. Wouldn't she have said something if she knew he had been here? Would she have been so excited to be invited by the Jordanian Ministry of Antiquities to organize a traveling exhibition?

"I don't believe you." I clench my fists, my hope shriveling.

"In café, I keep Mr. Steepp brown bag."

Dad's briefcase? My head swims and hope pours out like a waterfall. "Can I see it?"

"No time. Go now." Faisal's eyes are wide with fear. He tugs on his kiffiyah. "Hotel."

I follow the direction of his eyes and see Mr. Hasan talking to Double-Wide under a large awning, which shades the outdoor café next to the museum. I gasp. Their heads are bent toward each other as if they don't want anyone to overhear. Mr. Hasan must be part of the smuggling ring…and…and could he know what happened to Dad? Thoughts crowd my brain. After the memorial service, I refused to believe Dad was dead. Dead people have bodies to prove it. But he never came home, dead or alive. If he was alive, I am two hundred percent certain he would come home. I hurt so much that Mom took me to a counselor to talk about Dad, and help me accept Dad's death. I don't want to see that doctor again. Maybe Faisal has Dad confused with someone else, or has the date wrong. How would Faisal know Dad went off into the desert? How would he know bad men are looking for Gordy and me?

I exchange glances with Gordy and wonder if Faisal is making up stories. There's only one way to find out. A second source. My gut tells me Mr. Hasan is keeping secrets from me. I'm going to find out what. I hold up my hand, using my two fingers to walk across my open palm. Gordy nods.

I wait for a tour group to pass in front of our hiding spot so that I can slip into the knot of people. Gordy is on my heels. The group follows the path along the length of the museum, heading for the front. When the group turns left toward the museum entrance, I duck behind a large stone block the size of a car, which rests in the middle of the dirt path. The stone forces traffic to divert to the left or right. Everyone is looking at their feet because the path is uneven. I decide to climb on top for the perfect place to spy.

"No touch," Faisal yells drawing stares from tourists.

Startled, I jump back and Gordy throws his hands in the air like someone is holding a gun to his back.

"Why not?"

"Djinn block, bad luck. Door to dead."

Both Gordy and I move away from the djinn block into another group of tourists. I look toward the café where Mrs. Brown has joined Double-Wide and Mr. Hasan. Double-Wide has his back to us, but Mrs. Brown and Mr. Hasan are looking in our direction.

Crouching low, Gordy and I duck in behind four tourists posing behind an unfurled German flag. I don't think Mrs. Brown or Mr. Hasan saw us, but wonder what the Germans will think when they look at the photo and see four heads and twelve feet. Maybe the extra body parts will remind them of the Ancestor statue. We could use some ancestral protection right now since Faisal ruined my plan to eavesdrop. I wonder if he did that on purpose.

We use the tourists as a screen and return to Faisal.

I have so many questions; I don't know which one to ask first. About Double-Wide, Mr. Hasan, my dad or the Golden Girdle.

"We go up and wait till safe." Faisal points.

I follow his finger to the highest peak in all of Petra. It looks like a trap. There would be nowhere to hide or escape once we reached the top. I look back at Mr. Hasan and Mrs. Brown. She's shaking her finger at him, and his face is turning bright red. It would buy me more time with Faisal. Time to ask him about my dad. And maybe, the red mountains Faisal first told us about do hold the secrets of a hidden treasure.

I twist a braid around my neck while I think about leaving Mrs. Brown in Mr. Hasan's hands. I feel a twang of guilt because I haven't treated her very nicely by running off when she's the only one worrying if I'm okay. "Gordy, should we warn your mom about Mr. Hasan and Double-Wide?"

Gordy watches for a moment before answering. "I think...I think Mother can take care of herself. Let's get out of here." He pulls his laughing camel cap down low, but not before I notice his ears are bright red.

Faisal scrambles up between the boulders. There are no signs, or even a clear path.

Leaving Mrs. Brown behind, I realize no one knows where we are. Can I trust Faisal? I have images of him taking us to a far off place in the mountains, seeing djinn and leaving us to die of hunger and thirst. Why'd we have to get such a superstitious guide? One mention of spirits and he's gone. Like Dad. My gut tells me to follow Faisal, but I'm not sure if that means I can trust him, or that it's telling me it's time to get some answers.

SWEET TEA AND
CODED MESSAGES

The steps up the mountain are uneven and narrow. Dad would call it a one-butt trail. There are no tourists going up this path; plenty of locals are heading down. Each time they pass, we must squeeze our bodies against the rocks in an effort to create more space.

"*Bellaboooozzz!*" a Bedouin says, bounding by me.

Sweat drips down from under my hat and through my shirt. I don't think I look very bella at this point so he must mean someone else. I glance up the trail at Gordy. He's with Faisal talking non-stop. Doesn't he ever breathe?

Panting for air, I let my thoughts drift back to Dad and his secrets. The locked desk. The phone calls he'd take outside in the garden, even when it was raining. The long business trips. I'd ask about them and receive a vague answer. Or a story I suspected wasn't quite true. Was his death just a story? I close my eyes and remember the memorial service. The men with black suits. Mom crying as one of them, a Mr. Gray, dropped to his knees in front of me, telling me to take care of my mom, maybe call a relative to come and stay for a while. I kept asking where Dad's body was. He kept asking me if I knew if Dad had a secret hiding place. Or if I knew where he kept a special key, a small one, gold in color. I didn't tell him anything because he didn't tell me where Dad was. No one would tell me what happened. I felt like it was a plot, to keep Dad away from me. I didn't trust those men.

My eyes focus again on Gordy and Faisal, their heads bobbing together as they walk. Gordy stops and scoops up some discarded paper, shoving it in his backpack. How do I know I can trust them? Gordy blabbed to Mrs. Brown about the Golden Girdle. Faisal, maybe he's just in it for the money. Why else would he have come back? I wish Dad was here to tell me what to do.

"Faisal! Stop. Tell me what my dad was doing here."

Faisal turns and looks down the trail, but not at me. I look. In the distance I see Double-Wide's green police uniform. He's following us up the trail.

"No stop."

"Where are we going," I holler between gasps, trying to catch up to them.

"Up. We hide at Monastery. Yes?"

"How do you know the way?" I call up.

"Follow cairns."

"Corns? What corns?" I search, but see no plants, let alone vegetables. Just a blur of rocks.

"Cairns. See rocks up ledge? Trail markers."

I notice them for the first time. Three rocks piled one atop the other. Once I start paying attention, I spot the stacked rocks every time the path splits. I decide to memorize the route in case Faisal deserts us. Dad's Rule Number 5: learn the lay of the land.

"My dad," I holler again. "What did he tell you?"

"Mr. Steepp looking for people."

"Who? Did he find them? Where?"

"Looking for kids."

The path rises straight up through the rock now, and I'm not sure I heard Faisal right. The steps rise alongside a series of channels cut into the side of the cliff. The waterways Mr. Hasan told us about. I want to ask Faisal more questions, but I have no breath. It takes all my strength to put one foot in front of the other and climb. I don't want to fall behind because Double-Wide is gaining on us. The sun burns through my hat and brain. No thoughts make sense. Images of Faisal blur with Mr. Hasan and Dad. The memory of Double-Wide's worry beads clacks in my ears. I climb faster to get away from them, only to hear Mrs. Brown asking me to show her my backpack. I slow down to protect Mom's treasure. The pack feels like it weighs two hundred pounds. Sweat pours off me until my sneakers slosh.

My water bottle is finished. I don't care because a full bottle would weigh too much. My feet move. Faisal stops to look back down the mountain, checking for Double-Wide? Or djinn? One hour passes and then another, according to my watch. I think it lies; I am certain I have been fighting this mountain for days.

My vision clouds and clears like a sandstorm moving through. I see a tent. At first it's a blob, but then the sharp lines and angles of the brown canvas cuts into the startling blue sky. It's a dream. A mirage? I've read about them. Next I'll see water and a palm tree.

The ground is flat now. The tent bigger and more solid. I feel like I can reach out and touch it. I extend a finger, expecting the mirage to disappear at any second. Instead I feel coarse cloth scratch my finger.

We are on top of the mountain. Faisal leads us into a Bedouin encampment, a tent constructed of blankets and sticks, something a kid might build in the backyard and call a fort. A woman in a black robe covered with tiny cross stitches of red and green thread hunches over a fire cooking a brown lump which smells like bread. In my hazy brain, I wonder if they are Nabateans. It doesn't fit my idea of Queen Huldu's palace, but maybe she owned an upscale tent. Faisal greets an old man in Arabic. He wears a red-and-white kiffiyah like Faisal's. The old man spreads a wool blanket on the rocks, motioning us to sit. I collapse, still unsure if the camp is real. The woman hands me a cup of tea. Hot tea. I smile and shake my head. I'm sweating enough. I want to tell Faisal we need to talk.

Faisal is looking down the mountain. He smiles. "He turn back. Rest now." He makes a tsking sound at the untouched tea and me. "Drink. Hot tea make body cold."

Yeah, right, I think, bringing the tea to my lips.

The warm, sweet taste slides over my tongue and through my body like a spring rain. To my amazement, the world settles in my vision, no longer wispy and fleeting. Sipping the tea, I look around for the first time.

"Monastery." Faisal indicates toward a building three stories high, carved into the rock face. "No go inside. Bats."

I don't need any encouragement to stay where I am even through the blanket is scratchy and the rocks underneath jagged. I drink my tea and look out over the cliffs and across the vast desert. I'm sitting on the roof of the world.

"The Red Sea." Faisal waves toward the body of water off on the horizon. "Other side, Egypt."

I point to a bluish dome on the cliff below to my left, my throat feels too coated with sand to speak.

"Tomb of Aaron," Faisal says.

Aaron, like in the Bible? That would be one old tomb. Moving as slowly as the old woman making bread, I dig around in my backpack for a pair of miniature binoculars so I can take a closer look. The neck cord is stuck to the glossy paper with the picture of the zodiac and tangled in the muslin cloth hiding Mom's smelly blob. I take them all out and spread them on the blanket to disentangle them. This is a mistake because Gordy has sticky fingers.

"Give it back," I demand when Gordy grabs the piece of glossy picture of the Nabatean zodiac.

"When did you copy this?" Gordy points at the pencil markings around the zodiac.

"I didn't. Mom must have." The minute the words are out of my mouth I realize my mistake. Mom meant this to be a secret.

"Cool. She can write Nabatean."

I look at Gordy.

He points to the symbols. "It's the writing system I saw in the museum."

"So now you're an expert?" I say.

"Yeah," Gordy brags. "Okay, maybe not an expert, but I won every game I played on the translation board." Gordy digs in his backpack and pulls out a brand new pen, still in the cardboard container. The backpack looks as spanking new as his red sneakers. Then his beat up pack of cards falls out.

"Give me some paper from your journal," Gordy says.

I protect my backpack from his grabby hands. "Find your own paper. My journal is private."

He removes a crumpled piece of paper from his pack and spreads it out across his knee. It's one of the pieces of trash he picked up, a flyer with a picture of a kid with Arabic writing underneath. It's not the same kid as on the paper the lady gave me in the souq. This boy looks a little older. Gordy flips the paper over to the blank side, closes his eyes and is still a moment. I reach for the deck of cards, but Gordy is faster.

"That's mine." He returns them to his pack.

"I wasn't going to steal it."

"I know. I don't like people messing with my deck. It's the only thing that's mine."

Just when I think I'm figuring him out, he does something weird. Faisal and I watch as he writes the alphabet on the backside of the flyer. Skipping A, he draws a sideways U, with the top leg of the U curving up rather than ending even with the bottom leg. He skips the C, and under D he draws an upside-down L. He skips E and F, but under G he draws a Y resting on its side. The letters look more like cursive writing than printing, with rounded turns, not sharp angles. Gordy works through the entire alphabet. He gives it one last check and grins.

"It's like playing cards. You just got to memorize the order and keep count."

"What happened to the 'A', and the other letters you skipped?" I say.

"I told you. The Nabateans didn't have any written vowels. They also don't have all of our letters. The vowels, you just have to guess."

"Can you guess what Mom's doodles mean?" I ask. Overhead, an eagle circles in a slow loop hunting for prey.

Gordy takes the glossy paper with the pencil markings and begins matching the symbols to his chart. With each letter translated, Gordy gets more frustrated. "It's not working like it did in the museum."

I look at the letters, a bunch of gibberish. My stomach twitches. Dad always said gibberish to one person is code to another. Did Mom leave me a coded message?

"Let me try." I take Gordy's chart and the glossy paper. Mom thought Dad and I were just wasting time when we challenged each other to break codes. Dad broke mine in minutes. Sometimes it would take me days to figure out his. But I'd find the pattern. I always did. My brain works in patterns. He taught me to pay attention to repeat letters, because the letter E was used more than any other in the English alphabet. But there are no vowels in this code. Gordy tried the transliteration method, which is one form of simple substitution. Mom's no math whiz. She'd stick with substitution. Knowing Mom, however, she wouldn't mess up their alphabet.

"Is that the right order of the alphabet?" I point to Gordy's row of Nabatean letters.

"I lined up the sounds—"

"No, I mean *their* order. Like we always start with A when we write our alphabet."

"No, but I remember it." Gordy starts a fresh line, drawing the letters from left to right across the page.

I study the paper. There are twenty-two Nabatean letters. That means twenty-two possible variants for simple substitution. I don't have time to try twenty-two different possibilities.

Unless....

I find scissors and a ruler in my backpack. "Help me make a code wheel. Cut the cardboard that came with your pen into two circles, one a little bigger than the other," I tell Gordy.

Using the ruler, I take the bigger circle and draw two lines to cut the circle into quarters. Then I quarter the quarters, and quarter them again until I have twenty-six lines. I do the same thing on the smaller circle.

"Write the Nabatean alphabet around the smaller circle," I tell Gordy. "Keep the order right and when you run out of letters, start repeating from the beginning."

"You do what, Miss Ana?" Faisal peers over my shoulder.

"Breaking a code. Now get out of my light." I add a *please* when Faisal looks hurt.

"I take glasses? Yes?" Faisal asks. I look up to see him holding up my binoculars. Behind him, the old Bedouin stares off into the distance, reminding me of the hawk searching the rocks for movement. I nod and return my attention to the code wheel.

"Who taught you to break codes?" Gordy asks. I can feel his admiration.

"My dad."

Gordy grins. "Who taught him?"

I bite my lip and wonder why I never asked Dad that question. "Just help me finish this."

I write the English alphabet around the larger circle. Removing the yellow barrette from my hair, I break off the metal clasp. Gordy helps me poke it through the center of the two circles and bend it to pin the circles together. I rotate the circles, the larger one to the left and the smaller one to the right, so that the English A is lined up with the first letter of the Nabatean alphabet, which looks like an X with a broken foot.

"Now try to read it," I tell Gordy.

After a few minutes, Gordy shakes his head. "It didn't work."

I shift the inner wheel one letter to the left. The English Z is now lined up with the X with a broken foot. "Try again."

Gordy writes down the letters as he goes. He doesn't quit after a few letters, but speeds up, double-checking the wheel, before laying down his pen.

"Do I need to shift it again?" I take the wheel back.

Gordy shakes his head. His blues eyes look golden as the sun throws off its late afternoon colors. "We did it!"

A Clue and a Map

The Nabatean Pantheon will reveal itself from the top of the monastery. At the heart is the key. Follow the map to 'Uzza's lost shrine. Find the Golden Girdle and me.

That's not exactly how it looks, since the Nabatean alphabet is short four letters, making repeats necessary. Gordy has trouble figuring out what English letters to use in these cases, so "will" comes out as "aill" and "reveal" as "rezeal." Plus the punctuation is missing, but my brain figures it out. I take the pen and make the corrections. Then it hits me. Mom went to a lot of trouble to create and hide this secret note for me. She wants me to find the Golden Girdle…and her. Not as a treasure hunt. My skin prickles cold in the hot air. Mom's in some sort of trouble. I think about the note wrapped around the package, which sounded odd when I first read it. She said I would be reading it if she was detained.

Not delayed.

I'm the one with cooked brains. How could I not see she was calling for help?

"What do we do now?" Gordy asks.

Danger and urgency fight in my gut. Should I trust Gordy? What should I say? Mom's been kidnapped? Mom's given me clues? I think about how much time I've wasted thinking Mom had abandoned me. How much more time does Mom have?

"Follow the clue. We have to find this Nabatean Pantheon. Now."

We both look around our resting area. The only pantheon I know is in Greece, and it's a columned temple dedicated to the gods. It's full of carvings and statues. There's nothing like that on top of this mountain. The tomb is carved into the rock face, with the large door and fake windows. Other than an urn carved on top of the rock building, there are no sculptures or images of gods.

"Faisal, why do they call this place the Monastery?"

"Christian holy men call Monastery home. Believe Nabi Moses rested here."

"There are carvings of the gods inside?"

"No."

"But there's a special home around here, a pantheon for the Nabatean gods. Where is it?"

Faisal cocks his head, scratching his ear. "Petra home of Nabatean gods."

"Do you think we need 'Uzza's eyeball to see?" Gordy whispers.

I finger the cotton bundle from Mom. There's nothing about it that makes me think it might be 'Uzza's, unless 'Uzza suffered from stink-eye. Mom told me to keep it safe, so I'm not going to tell Gordy about it until I figure out why Mom gave it to me. Her life might depend on it. I put it back in my backpack and give Faisal another try. "Is there one temple for all the gods?"

He shakes his head. "One temple, one god. No sharing."

I groan. So much for Mom leaving one clear clue. I look to Gordy for ideas.

"Does 'Uzza have a shrine?" Gordy asks.

Faisal nods. "'Uzza is a goddess. Many places honoring her."

"Like where?" I demand. Can't Faisal ever give us a straight answer?

"By Colonnade is Temple of Winged Lions." He points down at a stone structure next to the row of columns, far below us, where we started our climb. He hands Gordy my binoculars. "Each god has shrine for worship. "'Uzza is big goddess and has big temple. Temple of Winged Lions biggest in all Petra."

I look down into the valley, squinting to make out the details of the temple, and decide the zoom lens on my camera would let me see more. I grab my camera from my backpack. That's when I feel something thrust in my hand. My camera's memory chip. I look at Gordy who's grinning.

"Your mom gave it back?"

"Not exactly," Gordy says. "I knew it was important to you, so I recovered it. Don't tell her."

Dad would have been impressed by Gordy's ability to lift stuff. Gordy's not as innocent as his blue eyes would make you believe. I'm keeping a close eye on my wallet around him. I peer into the camera viewfinder and zoom in on the temple. Three walls are still standing. The roof, if it had one, is gone. In the center of the building is a raised platform with a statue on it.

I put the camera down and let my eyes sweep the valley. It's like the mountains are cradled around it, to protect it from 'Uzza's enemies. Mom is somewhere down there, but where, 'Uzza isn't sharing. I panic at the size of the place, monuments appearing like toys and people like grains of sand. Mom could be hidden behind any of these rocky shields. So could the Golden Girdle.

The old man refills my cup of tea and smiles. He has no front teeth. He must be at least a hundred years old and sees everything that goes on from this perch in the sky. I grab my camera again and flip through the stored pictures. I find one of Mom posing next to a statue of an Egyptian goddess.

"Have you seen this woman?" I ask the old man, pointing at the picture, then two fingers to my eyes and then at him.

He takes his time looking at the picture. I pantomime my question again. He shakes his head.

"Ask him about 'Uzza and the Golden Girdle," Gordy says.

I decide Gordy has 'Uzza on the brain, but I'm running out of ideas of my own. I turn to Faisal. "You don't think he'd know about any ancient clues leading to the Golden Girdle?"

Faisal smiles and brings his hand to his heart, bowing his head to the old man, who sits by the fire warming his hands in the sweltering sun. To my surprise, he addresses him in English.

"Uncle, these friends, very best. They honor you and your fathers."

The old man smiles his toothless grin and brings his hand to his heart as well.

"Uncle, my friends wish to know of the Golden Horde. Uncle, tell us story of our land."

The grizzled man begins speaking. His voice is soft and musical. The English words flow easily, making me embarrassed I assumed he didn't understand anything we had said.

"Many came here seeking the Horde of the Golden Girdle, the riches of the greatest kings and queens. First the Romans. Then Persians and Turks. Now the Europeans come. They seek, but they do not find. You know why? Because treasure is cursed and will not reveal itself to anyone undeserving. It is said that he who seeks to restore the greatness of the Nabateans will be able to see through the eyes of Queen Huldu to the key of the Map of the Gods. Only 'Uzza's chosen can escape sand between the teeth."

I feel the magic of the words circling around me, painting images of kings and queens, riches and lost dreams. What would it have been like to live back then? I imagine walking among the Nabatean people. They would kneel, wanting my attention. I would be generous, giving gold and silver as rewards. No sand baths for my subjects. That would be my campaign poster. Water for all. As Queen, I'd be voted the best in all the land.

"Thank you Uncle. We go now," Faisal says, popping my fantasy and making the dreamy figures disappear. He has the binoculars again and is retracing our steps up the trail. Wrinkles line his forehead, and his knuckles are white against the black of the field glasses.

"Is someone coming?" I ask, remembering Mr. Hasan and the thieves.

He points to the setting sun. "We go down. Dangerous at night."

I have the weird feeling again, that it's not just the night he's afraid of.

A Grumpy God and
a Blocked Trail

Faisal herds us down the steps like it's a race. Gordy bounds in front of me. He must be part mountain goat. My legs protest but I try to keep up. I now understand what Mom meant when she would complain after a long day at a dig, climbing up and down the ladders into the pits until her legs felt like rubber.

I distract myself by finding shapes cut into the rocks by the wind and rain. I see cones and pyramids, all with weathered edges, smoothed over time. Two-dimensional shapes remind me of the polygons of my favorite game Blokus. Maybe Petra is one giant puzzle, and I just need to put the pieces together. Then it will tell me its secrets. Like where Mom is hidden. What about the Golden Girdle and her map? Is it the same one that the Bedouin mentioned—the map of the gods? My legs jolt and quiver with each step, especially when my foot slips on loose rocks. I grumble. Even if we had an ancient Nabatean map it wouldn't be much help. Only rubble remains.

I careen to a halt when I notice something doesn't fit: an outline of a block chiseled into the mountain. The edges are sharp, the sign of worked stone. The size of a grave marker, but there's nothing solemn about it. A silly face is carved in the center, with scowling eyes hooded by bushy eyebrows, pouting lips, and a nose long like a finger. Geometric script lines the base.

"What's this?" I shout at Faisal between gasping breaths.

Faisal pauses and glances back. "Shrine honoring warrior god al-Qaum."

Gordy has stopped too, examining the face up close. "You mean the grumpy god." He mimics the expression, making me laugh despite the heat and my gloomy thoughts.

Gordy crosses his eyes and lets his tongue hang out, which gives me an idea. "Faisal, are there more of these?"

Faisal hesitates. "Old stories say twelve shrines...I know ten or maybe eleven." He sounds distracted when he tells me about a block with a similar face in the Palace Tomb. Then he jerks back, pressing Gordy and me into the rock wall. He bites his lower lip.

"What? Did you see Mr. Hasan?" An urge to confront him and make him tell me what he's done with Mom rips through me. I press forward, but Faisal holds me back.

He points into the wadi at three figures. In the dimming light I see a man in a uniform. The clank of his worry beads echoes against the rock walls. The man with him makes Double-Wide look friendly. On Double-Wide's other side is a lady, Madam Isis. She's arguing with Double-Wide. Her hands create a language all their own as her red and gold dress swirls around her. I don't know where Madam Isis came from, but the thieves must have gotten tired of climbing and decided to wait for us to come back down.

"I stay. You go hotel," Faisal says.

Seeing Madam Isis reminds me Faisal still hasn't explained anything about my dad. I tell him I'm not going to the hotel, but Faisal's not listening.

"You take trail there." Faisal points to a goat track leading off to the left. A cairn marks it otherwise only a goat would notice it. "Follow the head and back of camel. After hump, right to hotel. Meet in morning. Seven at Haddad's House of Hummus. The father of my father master of cafe. We talk then."

"What about Mrs. Brown?" I search for her hat in the shadowy dots of people far below. She's must be worried about us by now. We've been gone hours, long past the time we were supposed to be back at the hotel. I also don't see Mr. Hasan. Has he done something to her?

Faisal pushes me toward the goat track. "Hotel."

Faisal does not stick around to get approval for his plan. But one more look at Double-Wide and Madam Isis convinces me it's not such a bad idea. Gordy and I head up the goat trail. Faisal was right about the path following an outline of a camel. However, he didn't mention he was sending us the long way. Up and down, up and down the mountain we climb, tracing out the head and ears of the camel. My knees feel like jelly. At every split in the path, Gordy waits for me to catch up and tell him which way to turn. I draw the outline of the camel, but he can't envision the lines in the dirt. Gordy is not Nabatean guide material.

We proceed down the neck, straight down. Gordy is still bouncing around, like he could go forever. Maybe his knobby knees are meant for mountains. Mine aren't. I groan in relief when we reach the flat ground of the wadi. It's almost dark and most of the tourists have left. At the base of the camel's hump, we start an uphill climb. We round a ledge, and I halt. Our trail has met up with a main path. Guards usher a group of tourists out of a cave opening and down cut steps into the valley below. A wooden sign is posted outside the cave.

Palace Tomb. Archaeologists at Work.

My heart quickens. Is this where Mom was working? Maybe she left a clue. I dash into the opening and into darkness.

A Stone Shrine and a Royal Offering

I hear Gordy telling me to wait up. He slips something cold into my hand. A flashlight. My pack is stuffed with important stuff, like my journal, colored pencils, a reflecting mirror and binoculars, but I never thought to bring a flashlight. I press the button; the cavern fills with light.

The tomb has two pits dug in the floor with wooden ladders leading down. The ladders look like they date from Huldu's time. Around the pits, archeologists have set up work tables, with high-powered lamps attached to a generator. Crates are stacked on one side, ready to hold uncovered artifacts. There are no signs of Mom.

Together, Gordy and I slip around the pits to a crack of an opening on the far side. We peer into another chamber, this one with square corners and carved walls. We squeeze through to explore. The walls appear painted with a swirl of reds, yellows and pinks. I finger the wall, expecting a smooth finish, but sandstone crumbles beneath my touch.

The final rays of daylight beam through a carved doorway opposite us, giving me a view of the top of the Treasury and the ledge with the urn where I saw Faisal perched earlier. Two Antiquities policemen march up the path toward us so I pull back. I hope they can't see us in the shadows of the tomb.

"Let's go back to the other room," I whisper.

Dimming the flashlight, we sneak back through the crack and creep along the wall to avoid the pits.

"There's another opening." Gordy points to scaffolding around a hole in the wall.

Inching up to it, I realize it is more like a window than a door. A square stone rests on the floor next to the scaffolding. I feel a tingle deep inside me when I touch the carved shrine with a god face next to the window. That's two we've found.

I shine the flashlight into the void and catch my breath.

Carvings of people and animals decorate the walls. The sandstone has worn away, but their outlines are still clear. On one wall a man and woman sit on carved thrones, and tiny people are positioned at their feet. The little people are holding out offerings: birds, animals, and lumps of something. The woman wears a crown on her head. She's staring at me with a smile on her lips like she's happy to see me.

"Who is she?" I say.

Gordy pushes his head into the hole next to mine. "She looks like a queen. Maybe she's one of your royal ancestors." Gordy flashes a grin in the trail of light.

I ignore Gordy's teasing. "Her subjects brought presents. Let's check out those lumps."

"Frankincense or myrrh. Remember what Madam Isis said."

I'd forgotten about that. I crawl through the opening for a closer look at the queen. I feel like one of the people at her feet. What can I offer as tribute? I'm fresh out of frankincense and myrrh. I stand there lost in my thoughts, imagining what life must have been like when Gordy tugs on my shirt.

"We should go."

"Why?"

"I was thinking those guards might return. I don't think we're supposed to be here, at least not after dark." Gordy has picked up a second flashlight from somewhere and is waving the beam toward the hole in the wall.

"You can, if you want. I'm staying. I have a feeling—"

"About the curse?" Gordy says.

"No! What if this is Queen Huldu? We should make an offering. What do you have in your backpack?"

Unlike mine, Gordy's pack is stiff and shiny, like it hasn't been used much. He pulls out trash, collected from the street. A queen would expect more. What would a Nabatean queen think valuable? I grab the pack, sorting through the contents in the bottom, finding his half empty water bottle. I ignore Gordy's protests. I pour it out on the dirt floor. The water doesn't puddle like I expect, but begins to spread out in a thin line away from the Queen. The line of water turns right, like it is going around a corner and then makes another turn and another. It comes to a stop after marking out a square shape in the floor.

"Cool," Gordy says.

I'm not examining the dirt any more, but the Queen. "She's looking at me."

"Guess she likes your offering."

I run my finger along the water track. The dirt moves away, and I touch rock. The water is seeping along a crack in the stone. Using my hands as a broom, I brush away the dirt. Gordy drops to his knees and helps. The floor is solid stone, except in one area where a piece has been cut out and then replaced. I curl my fingers around the edges of the stone and try to move it. Gordy reaches for the two other corners.

"One, two, three. Lift!" I say. Gordy groans loudly, but it doesn't budge.

I study the Queen's face. It's in profile, but the eye is carved straight on. It's peering down at an angle.

"I was thinking, what if you have to push some secret place on the wall to open the stone in the floor. You know, like in the movies," Gordy says.

"Help me up," I say. Every now and then this kid's got a good idea. I motion for Gordy to get down on all fours so I can climb up. He hesitates, and then drops to the ground. I lock both hands around his forehead. I wrap my legs over his shoulders. Gordy struggles to stand with me riding piggyback. The first attempt he rams me into the wall, causing me to lose my grip. I pick myself up and give him my most she-devil look. The next time he drops to his knees and braces his hands against the wall. I climb up again, and then Gordy pushes up to a standing position.

"Okay, now crab slowly over to the Queen."

"What?" Gordy says. He sounds like a weightlifter groaning as he heaves a truck, but his feet start moving. With five more steps I reach the Queen. But I'm not tall enough to reach her eye.

"I'm going to balance on your shoulders," I say.

Ignoring his groans, I grab his head and pull my leg up. Gordy's shoulders are narrow, making it hard to find good footing. So I sit back down and remove my sneakers and socks.

"Peeeeuuuw." Gordy scrunches his eyes and nose.

"I call it Eau de Toe Jam. Like it?"

I wiggle my toes; they are happy to be free of my sweaty sneakers. I get one foot up, then the other. I am squatting, feeling like a frog on a lily pad bobbing in the water.

"Stay still."

I straighten my legs. I can't help but put my hands on the wall to steady myself. I apologize to the King when I knock a bit of him off. Sandstone is named sandstone for a reason.

I balance eye to eye with the Queen. I press my fingers into the center of her eye, and wait to hear the sound of the stone moving. I turn to look back down at the outline of water, when I see a flash of movement in the next chamber.

I can't make out the face, but something metal glints. A gun.

A Secret Cache and
a Broken Treasure

When I come to, bright shapes swim around my head. Some people see stars. I see polygons—squares, trapezoids, triangles, zees, and kites.

"Please don't die," I hear Gordy mutter from far away.

Something is dragging me by the foot. The stone scrapes my skin like a giant Brillo pad. I kick my foot free, but that makes the polygons explode in my head. "Owwww."

"Thank you. Thank you. Thank you. I promise I'll be good the rest of my life. I'll never steal again. I promise."

Through a crack in my eyelids I fix on Gordy, paper white, looking down at me.

"You trying to kill me?" I roll on my side and brush the sand out from under my T-shirt. My head feels like it grew and is now too heavy for my neck.

"You fell...you wouldn't wake up...men...fight... dead...I didn't know...run...stay... back..." Gordy spews out words, none of them making any sense.

I force myself into a sitting position and lean against the wall. It's dark. Filtered light glows from within Gordy's backpack. It's like it swallowed a light bulb. The shapes in my head lose their blinding color, and my eyes focus. I'm still in the Queen's tomb. "What happened?"

"You slipped and hit your head." Gordy sits opposite me, his eyes moving from me to the window in the wall and back.

I close my eyes. I remember I was perched on Gordy's shoulders, head to head with the Queen. I wanted to view the tomb from her perspective. My eyes pop open, and I see the faint outline on the floor. The water has almost dried up.

"How long was I out?"

"Too long. I was afraid you...you..."

"Gordy Brown. It takes more than a tumble to kill me." I try to sound indignant, but I'm pleased he was worried.

"There was a man—"

As soon as Gordy says this, I remember the man and the gun. I gasp, and my polygons swarm. Good thing I'm not standing up.

"The gun! What happened?" I say once I control the urge to barf.

Gordy forgets to talk slow. He tells me how a man with the gun started to climb through the window, but stopped when other men arrived. He didn't know how many, but there was a fight. The gun fired, but the fighting continued. They hollered in Arabic. Gordy said one voice sounded different from the others. More clipped and refined. Then it was quiet.

My chin drops. I can't believe I missed all that. "Are they gone?" I whisper.

Gordy nods. "It's been quiet for a long time. I was thinking I should get help, but then I'd have to leave you alone. What if they were there and caught me…"

"They didn't come in here?" I say, a little louder.

"No. I shut off the flashlights and pushed you into a corner. Maybe the other men didn't see us. But the man with the gun…"

No wonder I have sand in my pants. Gordy has been dragging me around like an overstuffed book bag.

Then I think about the cut stone in the floor and what might be under it. Someone was trying to beat me to it. Dad's Rule Number 6: suspect everyone.

"So no one tried to open the stone in the floor? Not them? Or you?" I look at Gordy because I've turned on my lie detector. It might not be as good as Mom's, but Gordy's not a professional liar, like me.

Gordy flushes. "I thought you were dead, and those men would kill me too!" He yanks his laughing camel hat out of the back pocket of his shorts and pulls it down over his eyes. He puts his back toward me, arms crossed.

He doesn't say anything. It may be the longest time in his life he hasn't spoken. I wonder what he's thinking. In the silence, I hear my heart beating. If those men had come in here, maybe it wouldn't be. "Thanks," I mumble.

Gordy shifts away further. He pulls out his cards and shuffles.

I know Gordy saved my life. But I can't let him be angry at me for thinking about why we are here in the first place. "Don't be mad. Listen. I now understand what that Bedouin meant about Queen Huldu and the map of the gods."

Gordy's head turns a quarter of an inch toward me.

"It's a puzzle. Mom said 'Uzza will lead us to a map. Madam Isis said 'Uzza protects Queen Huldu's jewels from treasure hunters who don't deserve to find them. Maybe the map is a treasure map meant to be discovered by the rightful heir of Queen Huldu—"

"The Bedouin said only he who seeks to restore the greatness of the Nabateans will be able to find the key of the Map of the Gods."

"Or she."

Gordy faces me. "He and she?"

"She and he."

Gordy grins.

I glare. "This isn't a game. We've got to figure this out." I point at the wall carving. "If this is Queen Huldu, she's staring at that stone in the floor. The key must be hidden there."

Gordy rummages through his backpack. When he doesn't locate what he is searching for, he dumps it out on the floor, half-eaten orange and all. The juice has soaked into Tomb Robber's envelope, disintegrating one side. Out falls the drawing of 'Uzza's eye, a photograph of his mom, and a package of boy's underwear, still in its plastic wrap, a flashlight, and his hotel room key. Like mine, it is an old fashioned key attached to a large metal orb with his room number inscribed in extra large type. Dad told me they made them big so travelers wouldn't forget about them and pocket them by mistake when they check out.

While Gordy roots around, I pick up the sticky photograph. Mrs. Brown has a don't-mess-with-me face on, not a smile. "I thought she didn't like her picture taken? You don't look much like her. With her hair pulled back in a ponytail, she kind of looks like my mom."

Gordy glances at the photo and frowns. I expect him to say something, like listing the entire genealogical chart of his family, but he doesn't. Instead he studies the Swiss Army knife in his hand. Then I remember he hasn't yet met my mom.

I try to take the knife from him, but he blocks me. "What about the curse?"

I swallow. I'm not sure if I believe in curses, but I wouldn't want to find out the hard way. "Let's swear to use the treasure for the benefit of the Nabateans. Anyway, my mom wouldn't allow me steal any artifact. She'd blow her top." I think about the crab disk and pray to all the gods in the pantheon that I'll see her again, even if it means a scolding.

"Okay, but sometimes people have good reasons for taking stuff."

I stare at Gordy, uncertain what he means. Protecting only works so far. He pulls out one of the short blades and runs it along his arm as if looking for a special spot.

"What are you doing?" I ask.

"Making a blood pledge."

Gross. I'd rather not give 'Uzza any ideas. "We already have a slap swear. Let's just add to it."

Our cheeks stinging once again, we swear the treasure will go to the museum. In my mind, I'm seeing Mr. Hasan. No way am I handing the Map of the Gods or the Golden Girdle over to him. I wonder if Gordy is thinking of exceptions too.

We take turns with Gordy's knife breaking the dirt seal holding the stone in place. Even though the stone is the size of my backpack, it takes us a long time to pry it loose. I mean hours. My imagination is running away with dreams of treasure spread among plates of hamburgers, macaroni and cheese and hummus. I lose track of time, but I begin to suspect we're closer to morning than night. What will happen if daylight comes, and tourists come into the Palace Tomb expecting to find archaeologists at work, as the sign said outside? I look at Gordy. We'd be doomed. He looks more like a tomb robber than an archaeologist in those now dusty red sneakers. I grab my pack of special color pencils. This is an emergency. Dad would understand. I select my least favorite color, pink, and start scraping. The two of us working together speeds up the process, but my dreams now feature more food and less gold.

Broken pencils litter the floor: pink, purple, yellow, dark green, orange, gray and red. Only the blues, the black and my favorite mint green are left when Gordy abandons his knife because the blade is too short to reach the remaining dirt seal. Without a word I offer him a choice of blues. That's a mistake. Gordy hems and haws over which color would be better, sky blue or navy, until I throw both at him. We keep digging like we are tunneling to China with a plastic spoon. Long ago, I stopped feeling everything except my head throbbing in time with my pencil jabbing.

I am pushing the black pencil up and down in the dirt when I realize it isn't in my hand. It has slipped down into the crack. I hear it dance to a standstill below.

"Listen. It echoed like there's a cavity under there!" My exhaustion disappears with the pencil. "The key must be in there. How are we going to lift the stone?"

My fingers are numb. I suspect Gordy's are also. I don't remember seeing any tools left on the archeologists' tables. Dad always told me necessity is the mother of invention. I dump my backpack out, next to Gordy's, everything except for my journal and the muslin bundle. That's private. In the glow of the flashlight, we discard items…my hairbrush, binoculars, the code wheel, the pack of color pencils, two black markers, a plastic keychain reproduction of Munch's Scream from the Metropolitan Museum of Art, an embroidered pouch with a cord my dad brought back from a business trip to Morocco, and a zippered bag with the New York subway system map on it.

"What's in here?' Gordy fingers the zipper.

"That's personal." I grab at the bag. But before I can snag it, he has my compass, mirror for signaling, and my prized pen with invisible ink. "Give that back."

"What's this stuff for?"

"Gifts from my dad. Special memories from when he was…at home."

Gordy hands back the bag and picks up an elastic headband. The pink band has been in the bottom of my backpack since forever. Mom bought me a pack of three for soccer practices. I wore the black one once, my first and last day at practice. I left it on the field along with my pride. Some things are harder than they look. Gordy stretches the band over his head.

"I don't think it's your color."

"Is there another one?" Gordy says, returning to my pile.

I dig around in an outer pocket of my backpack and find a matching yellow band. This one has little red hearts on it. I'm too interested in watching Gordy to feel embarrassed. He takes the pink headband and the navy pencil and stretches the band down and around one corner of the stone. He is trying to hook the hair band on the bottom of the stone.

"Got it," he says, his grinning camel bobbing in glee. He removes the pencil and begins pulling the band along the crack toward the other corner.

ZAP.

Pink flies up and hits the King in the face. Sand particles chip away, leaving a dust pile on the floor next to the escaped hair band.

Gordy recovers the band and starts over. This time I help, using my mint green pencil to hold the band in place on the first corner. Despite a tight stretch, we fix both the pink and yellow bands around the width of the stone plug.

"Okay, now what?" I say.

"We lift straight up and shove our feet underneath the stone it to keep it from resealing."

I look down at my feet. My shoes are missing. I remember taking them off to climb on Gordy's shoulders, but where did I throw them? "What if there are scorpions down there? It might not be safe with bare feet."

"It would be cool to see a real, live scorpion," Gordy says.

"Yeah, well not when one stings you." I clap my hands together several times.

"What are you doing?"

"I'm giving any scorpions in the hole a warning we are coming so they aren't surprised."

"So they like applause?"

"Any kind of noise works," I groan. He manages to make the simplest things complicated.

Gordy shakes his prized camel hat off, and I jam it in one corner like somehow that would stop the stone from falling back into its cradle. Still, it's better than losing my toes.

Standing with our heads butting, Gordy and I bend down on opposite ends of the stone. I lift up on the pink headband while Gordy grabs the yellow with hearts. We pull. The hair bands grow taut and skinny. I hold my breath hoping they won't break and put out my eye. We keep tugging. The stone begins to budge. An inch. My pink band is stretching more than Gordy's. The elastic threads start to fray by my right pinkie. The one I used to take the oath. Did 'Uzza read my thoughts about Mr. Hasan and decide to curse us after all?

"FASTER."

I yank, and Gordy does the same. The hair band snaps. I watch the pink tip slip from under the stone and bite into my right hand. The stone hangs in the air. Gordy jerks and slides, like he is going into home plate. I can't help since I'm flying backwards, freed from my hair band anchor. Dust sprays up in the air, obscuring my vision, but not my hearing.

Gordy lets loose a stream of swear words that would get me grounded for life. What kind of kids does he hang out with? He doesn't even try to cover them up with an apology, but continues swearing while nursing his right leg. I can see a reddish, purple mark move across his shin. The stone is resting on its side, next to the hole. Carved on the underside is a figure of a lady pouring something liquid from a vase. Another offering to the Queen?

"You shouldn't swear in front of royalty. You might make her angry." I pick myself up off the stone floor and peer into the cavity.

"Check for scorpions," Gordy says.

I recoil. "Maybe you should."

"Nope. You're the long lost and curse-proof daughter of Queen Huldu."

I open my mouth for a response, but can't think of one. Instead I flare my nostrils. Gordy laughs and hands me the flashlight. I doubt nostril flaring will work on scorpions, but I know what will.

I shine the beam down into the opening, a spotlight in a black hole. "They're nocturnal and sensitive to light." I shudder when I think about their little black hearts beating inside their black bodies, waiting for a chance to sting with their long bug

129

tails. My eyes focus on a thin black shape, and I instinctively pull the flashlight back. Gordy laughs at me. I give him the evil eye and lean over the hole again, inching the flashlight down closer to the opening. When it doesn't move, I realize it's my black pencil, wedged between a stone and something colorful. Sweat drips down my forehead as I reach in and touch cloth. Gordy is leaning over the cavity now too, pushing my head aside. He can shove all he wants because I hold the bundle in my hand, as I unwrap it with the other. The cloth is a delicate weave of red and gold silk.

Something glistens in the beam. It's gold like the crab disk, except it is much bigger and looks to be half of a woman's face.

No wonder 'Uzza is mad; someone broke her key.

A Dead Man and
a Live Curse

Gordy takes the gold piece from me while I keep the flashlight beam steady on it. "What is it?" Gordy says. With his finger, he traces the intricate grooves embossed into the gold.

"One weird looking key," I say.

Gordy pulls the crab disk from his pack and places it next to the half disk. "Do you think this is meant to go with the Crab?"

"No, it's not round."

"Maybe there's another half somewhere," Gordy says.

I grab the disk from him. "How are we supposed to find another half? It would be like looking for a needle in a haystack." I feel tears building. I was so certain the key would make everything clear, like it would have a note and arrow where to find Mom. I've wasted hours and am no closer to finding her.

"We'll figure it out," Gordy assures me. "We need to think through the clues." A loud rumbling deep in Gordy's stomach echoes in the tomb. "I'd think better with some food. We're supposed to meet Faisal soon. Maybe he can help...and feed us too."

We shove 'Uzza's key and everything else back into our packs and replace the stone in its cradle. I find my shoes. Then I make a promise to Queen Huldu to protect her gold key, even if it's useless to me, hoping she will spare us her wrath and leave us curse free. We mask our flashlights and crawl through the stone window. It feels like a lifetime ago that we discovered it. Across the pits, the early rays of daylight shine through the cave opening. We have been here all night, and Mrs. Brown must have sent a search party after us. If she was angry with Gordy after we ran off to the souq for a few hours, what would she be like now? I don't ask Gordy. I'm sure he knows he's in big trouble, no matter what. I pick my way around the work tables, making sure my feet don't stray too close to the edge of the pit. I glance into the depths and freeze mid-step.

"Not everybody left."

In the bottom of the pit, there's a man in a white suit. His head rests at an unnatural angle.

Gordy freezes too, but doesn't say a word.

I coil my braids around my neck as I back away.

"You should go down there and check on him. What if he's not dead? What if he is...? We have to be sure—" Gordy says.

"I can see just fine from up here." The man's suit is crumpled and covered with footprints, like he'd been walked on. Or kicked. I shudder when I remember this all happened with Gordy and me in the chamber next door. Then I spot his hand, draped across his chest. A silver snake ring climbs up his middle finger.

"It's Tomb Robber."

"Do you think 'Uzza got him?" Gordy's words come out in a sputter, like the last of the catsup from the squeeze bottle. "He's got dirt between his teeth."

"'Uzza's a lady goddess, and I don't believe she wears boots." Still, I feel a strong urge to toss the cursed key into the pit.

"He warned us." Gordy gets a faraway look but doesn't tell me what he's thinking. He lets the flashlight in his hand bounce throughout the cave. And then I see a glint of something in the dirt.

"Shine your light over there." I point. The light moves and I head for the spot where I swear I saw something shiny, all the while trying to avoid looking in the pit. Half buried in the dirt, with a dusty footprint over the top of it, is the golden lion. The disk Tomb Robber showed to the shopkeeper.

"It must have fallen out of his jacket during the fight," Gordy says.

"They're going to come back looking for it now that there's light. They'll want to come before the place opens, before someone finds the body and calls the police."

Maybe that's a good thing, because I don't plan on staying here. People are out there willing to kill for the clues he was carrying. If they suspected Gordy and I now have it, what would they do to us?

I lurch away from the pit "We can't talk to the police. They'll want to know why we were here. We can't tell anyone what we have discovered."

"But I was thinking—"

"No, we're in this together. No one."

Gordy's silent again.

"Mom's in trouble. Not busy, or missing, but serious trouble."

"My mother, Mrs. Brown…she's…she's not…"

The morning light begins to turn the rocks outside the tomb from shadows to golden reds.

"I know your mom will be worried or mad or both, but my mom's kidnapped or something worse."

"That's what I'm trying to tell you—"

"We have to get out of here, before someone sees us. We'll go to the café and meet Faisal; he'll know what to do."

"I was thinking—"

"What?" Doesn't he understand we don't have time for this?

"—we need to be careful about trusting what our mothers say."

I feel woozy again. Why doesn't Gordy trust my mom?

A Missing Guide
and a Golden Clue

We race through the near empty alleys of the souq. Sleepy-eyed merchants unlock shops and throw water from buckets onto the ground to clean the entryways. I find Haddad's House of Hummus, not making a single wrong turn. Its location in the maze of alleys is printed in my mind.

Gordy shades his eyes and peers into the darkened cafe. "No one's there."

I give the door handle another shake. Faisal said to meet him here at seven. We are early. We lean against the cool sandstone bricks, hiding in the shadows.

We wait fifteen minutes and then another thirty. Shoppers begin to appear and the air grows hot. Gordy asks me twice if I'm certain we are in the right place. We play cards in the shadow of the doorway. Gordy beats me in two games of Hearts. I refuse to play a third.

I watch the people going by and wonder if they are watching me. A man in a jalabiya lingers a little too long in the alley. I imagine I've seen him before. Is he an accomplice of Double-Wide? Or maybe he works for Mr. Hasan? He has the cruel face of a murderer. A toddler tumbles out of a shop, and the man scoops him up. I stand up preparing to shout for help. The child squeals in delight. The face is all smiles now as the toddler holds the man's little finger and pulls him inside the shop. I shake my head to stop my overactive imagination.

A boy in a uniform of blue shorts, white shirt and a red neck scarf walks toward us. I tell myself he's a Boy Scout or a Junior Ranger, no threat to me. I'm surprised when he stops right in front of me.

"For whom are you waiting?"

"Faisal." I am startled by his perfect British accent. "Our guide," I add, in case he thinks we need one. "He's supposed to meet us here."

"He is not coming."

"Yes he is. He promised."

The boy covers his face with his hands for a moment before walking away. I notice that despite the uniform and fancy English, he has on the same kind of tattered sandals Faisal wears.

"How do you know?" I call after him.

The boy stops and turns. "He has disappeared." I see fear in his eyes now. "He did not return home last night. Our

138

grandparents spent the night searching for him. We fear he has been taken like the others."

"Are you Ali, Faisal's brother?"

He nods, his pain written across his face. I can see he cares for Faisal as much as Faisal does for him.

"Maybe he stayed with friends." I am thinking about the Bedouin tent on top of the Monastery.

"No, bad men with the evil eye took him."

The image is replaced by the memory of Faisal's face when he saw Double-Wide with Madam Isis. Double-Wide fits my definition of a bad man with an evil eye. My mouth goes dry.

"Do not linger here; it is not safe." Ali runs away, disappearing into the flow of shoppers before I can stop him.

Gordy and I are alone once again. Gordy looks up and down the street, making me worry my imagination is not overactive. Dad's Rule Number 7: if it feels wrong, it is wrong. Where is Double-Wide? What has he done with Faisal? Does the market have eyes and ears, some of them evil? Sooner or later, someone will figure out where we are, and Double-Wide might come for us next.

Click. Clack. Click. Clack.

I hear the sound of worry beads echo off the confined pathways of the souq. Double-Wide. Why is it every time I think about someone, they suddenly appear?

"We need to hide." I look around at the locked shops.

"Hiding is my specialty," Gordy says.

"I'm not joking." I press my body into the wall of the café, hoping to disappear.

"Me neither."

I hear a click and turn to see Gordy holding the door to the cafe ajar. In his hand is his Swiss Army knife.

"How'd you do that?" I lean over to examine the lock.

"Can we talk about it inside?" Gordy looks one way and then the other before yanking me through the door.

We settle at a table in the back, away from the windows. Chairs are up on top of tables, and the polished floor gleams. Empty, the café looks twice the size it did yesterday. Gordy's stomach growls, echoing in the emptiness. I decide to explore the kitchen and return with pitas and salty cheese. My stomach is tight with worry. The food tumbles in my stomach like my thoughts: Tomb Robber who had a picture that looks like mom; the shopkeeper who offered to steal antiquities for him and the old man who served us lunch and shooed the shopkeeper away. I wonder if the old man was Faisal's grandfather. Now he's out looking for Faisal, who has been taken like the others. What others? Is Faisal in trouble because he helped us? Will Faisal tell Double-Wide we're hiding in this café? Is that why he sent us here? I look at Gordy who's snapping his knife open and closed. Even with the knife, Gordy doesn't look like he'd frighten anyone. But I'm learning looks can be deceiving.

"How'd you learn to pick locks?"

"I just popped it open, no big deal," Gordy says, not looking at me.

"And picking pockets?"

Gordy pretends not to hear me.

"Why are you so good at hiding?" I try again.

"It doesn't matter."

"Does your school have bullies?"

"Sure."

"Your friends help you hide?"

"I don't have friends," Gordy says at last, eyes hooded.

Private school. Figures. Full of snobs. My school's packed with them too. They think they're special. "Know what you mean. There's no one at my school who'd stay up all night with me digging up treasure with colored pencils. They expect their parents to buy them everything."

Gordy grins, folding the knife blade closed. "No one I know would do a slap swear not to steal."

We both laugh, though mine is forced at first. Something's bothering Gordy, and I wonder why he won't tell me. He seems a lot different from the kid I met in the cab in New York who couldn't stop talking. He also looks different. When we started this trip, his clothes were new, and he didn't seem to know much. Now he's covered with dirt, and I suspect he's been around more than he's letting on.

I reach into my pack and pull out the smelly package Mom hid. Gordy broke the code and helped me find the clue in the floor of the Palace Tomb. He saved my life. Maybe he can help save Mom's. If I can't trust him now, then when?

"Mom left me this." I unwrap the muslin cloth and hand Gordy the odd shaped blob. "I think it's a clue to the hiding place of the Golden Girdle."

He doesn't look the least bit surprised I've been holding out on him. He takes it and rolls it around in his hands. He holds it up to his nose and takes a big whiff. Then he licks it.

"That's disgusting. Give it back." I grab it and tug. Gordy doesn't let go right away. So I let go, but so does he. Mom's secret clue smacks down hard on the marble tile and shatters.

"NOOOO," I groan.

"It's just plaster," Gordy says.

"And you broke it!" I'm on my knees picking up the pieces of stinky fragments, wondering what I will tell Mom, assuming I could find her now that Gordy broke our clue.

Gordy takes the largest piece and begins picking off gray chunks. "Your mother must have mixed the plaster with dung and debris from the dig site. The stink alone would keep most people away." That's when I see the gold.

I stare at Mom's treasure. It's a golden disk, or half of one, and I've seen it before. It's part of a face like the one from Queen Huldu's tomb, now in the bottom of my backpack.

I dump the contents of my pack on the floor in front of me. I put to one side the paper with the decoded message from the ancient Nabatean letters and the first note Mom left me. I focus on the piece of cotton cloth holding the Crab disk Gordy pinched from the museum, the lion disk Tomb Robber left behind, and the larger half-disk we found in Queen Huldu's tomb. A thought flashes in my mind. Archaeologists aren't supposed to keep treasures for themselves. Gold is definitely a treasure. Where did Mom get it? Did she steal it? I shake the thought away. Mom doesn't steal. She doesn't lie. She doesn't even dissemble very well.

I take the two halves and try to fit them together, but globs of plaster still cover parts of my half. Gordy takes it from me and pulls out his pocketknife. He carves until the remaining plaster breaks off, leaving a pile of dust on the floor. The disk slides into place, locking into the other half. The pattern etched into the disk emerges; it's the head of a woman wearing a crown. I know I've seen this somewhere before. Think. Think. Then I remember. "Nike and the Nabatean Zodiac."

"What?"

"This is the head that sits in the center of the zodiac." Gordy still doesn't get it.

I arrange the crab and the lion disks in their proper places around the crown. I show him the picture of the zodiac Mom left with the muslin bundle. "We need to find this statue in the Temple of the Winged Lions. Before Mr. Hasan."

"Why Mr. Hasan?" Gordy says.

"Because Mr. Hasan has been trying to get rid of us since we arrived. He's covering up for my mom not being around. We're a problem. We shouldn't be here. He must be the imposter Mom warned me about. I bet he sent the fax ordering us not to come, not Mom."

"What fax?"

Right. Gordy and Mrs. Brown don't know about the fax. Now's not the time for confessions. "Never mind about that. Mom's in trouble."

"What imposter?" Gordy asks, his voice oddly high pitched.

"Mr. Hasan. He's got Mom, and he's lying about it."

"Why would Mr. Hasan want to kidnap your mother?" Gordy says slowly.

I wonder if his brain is overloaded, and his mouth is having trouble working. "Mom's a real expert. She knows more about Nabatean stuff than Mr. Hasan. That's why he kidnapped her. Mr. Hasan and his gang are already stealing treasures from the Petra Museum. You saw them in the basement. But Mr. Hasan wants the biggest treasure of the Nabateans."

"That doesn't make any sense. Your mother came here to borrow Nabatean art for an exhibition in New York."

144

I shake my legs, trying to contain my frustration. I should have figured this out two days ago. "This isn't about the exhibit, but the Golden Girdle. He brought her here with a story about putting together an exhibition for her museum. That's not what he wants. He wants the Golden Girdle, and Mom knows how to find it. Mr. Hasan knows she knows."

"You're not making sense."

"Mom published an article about the lost treasures of the Nabateans last year. Mr. Hasan must have read it. Mom didn't reveal the exact location, but she said she put in enough hints that when we uncover it, she could point to the article as evidence she solved the mystery from the ancient clues, not dumb luck."

"Where was it published?" Gordy asks. He looks sad. He has his cards out again, flipping the Queen of Spades. He's the one not making sense.

"*In Archaeology Yesterday and Today.* It's not something most people would read. There are no pictures. I didn't even read it, but that's not my point. Now I know how to find her."

"My mother gets that magazine." Gordy buries the black Queen and pulls out the Queen of Hearts.

Okay, so some normal people read it. I don't argue because I'm too busy watching the puzzle pieces snapping together in my brain. I hold up the flyer with the picture of the boy and the decrypted message on the other side.

The Nabatean pantheon will reveal itself from the top of the monastery.
At the heart is the key. Follow the map to 'Uzza's lost shrine. Find the
Golden Girdle and me.

"Put your cards away. We have to go back to the Temple of
the Winged Lions. 'Uzza's Temple."

"Is that 'Uzza's lost shrine?"

"I don't know, but it has to be connected."

"But what about the curse?" Gordy flips up the King of
Spades.

I think about the rumpled white suit in the bottom of the pit.
Dad used to tell me being afraid was okay because it makes you
think harder. "We still have our slap swear to Queen Huldu so
we should be okay. I have to find my mom."

"You think she's in the Temple of the Winged Lions?"

"No, silly. The woman holding the big disk over her head is
there."

Gordy is fidgeting. He grabs the photo of the zodiac. The
bottom of the page is torn and some of the type is worn so the
caption reads: *An an----t sun disk the Nabat--n's ---- -- - map -- the*
celestial -------r. ------ in the Temple of the ---ged Lions.

In a blink, polygons burst forward in my vision and
interlock.

Map. Everyone keeps talking about maps. Gordy's treasure
map. The map to 'Uzza's shrine. The map of the gods. Now a
celestial map? Can a map be round? Round like a disk. Round

like a zodiac? My gut tightens. The zodiac is 'Uzza's map to Petra.

The map to the Golden Girdle. And Mom.

THREE PASSPORTS
AND TWO PIGTAILS

Maps and treasure are swirling in my head while I search a small storeroom to the side of the kitchen. On top of a pile of Arabic newspapers are two white jalabiyas—exactly what we need. I've already borrowed two bottles of water. I hope Faisal's grandparents won't be sore if I take an emergency supply of clothing as well. I pull them off the shelf and make contact with a hard rectangular object.

"Find anything?" Gordy yells from the kitchen.

I don't say a word, but stare at the initials engraved on the clasp of a brown briefcase: JLS. I touch the release. My hand shakes. The case is locked. One by one, I rotate the dials of the lock, setting the first dial to a six, the second to a two and the third to a six. June twenty-six. My half-birthday. The lock clicks open.

"This is my dad's."

The words sound distant, like they came from someone else. I flip the case open and close my eyes. I smell leather and memories. When Dad returned home from trips, he would always hide a present in this case for me. What's it doing here? Did Dad give it to Faisal for safekeeping, like Faisal said? Or something else?

I reach my hand inside. There's a newspaper dated six months ago. I discover some of Dad's business cards and an unused airline ticket from Amman to New York. I feel weak in the knees and sit down fast. My head is swimming. This is the flight he should have taken, but didn't. There's something else. I hold up a paper heart. The cut out shape is jagged, the coloring messy. Written in red crayon is "I lov you Daddy." Breathing is hard. Tears slip down my face and drip onto the heart. I made it for Valentine's Day when I was in kindergarten. He always carried it with him...

"You okay?" Gordy kneels next to me.

"It's Dad's," I say, over and over again.

He was here. Faisal wasn't making it up. I turn the case upside down and let the rest of the contents pour out. Some coins, paperclips, writing pad and a pen. I pay no attention to these. I run my fingernail along the inside, behind the lock and clasp. I finger the small wire and push. Groping deeper, at the bottom seam, I do the same thing. This wire was always the hard one to find. It takes me three tries, but when I catch it, the bottom of the briefcase releases. This was our special hiding place. Where Dad hid my presents if they were small enough to fit inside.

I put my hand in the hidden cavity, discovering more paper and something metal. I pull out a key, passports and a clipping from a British newspaper. Three passports. I flip the first one open. I can feel Gordy's breath on my cheek. There's a picture of Dad, but the name is wrong. I open the second and find Dad wearing a beard with another wrong name. My hands are shaking too much now. Gordy helps, opening the third passport. It's blue, like the others, but with his name and picture.

"Why does your father have so many passports?"

"He travels a lot." I know that makes no sense at all. But I can only worry about one thing at a time. My attention is focused on the clipping. It's about missing kids. An organized crime group is stealing kids from countries around the globe, the British authorities say, and using them for illegal activities...smuggling, drugs in Asia, guns in Africa. In Dad's block letter handwriting there's a note down the right margin:

Israel: 3. Yemen: 13. Egypt: 10. Jordan: 45 (Petra 21).

What? Drugs? Antiquities?

Faisal said Dad was asking too many questions. Dad disappeared. So has Faisal. Does that change it to Petra: 22 or 23?

Gordy sucks in his breath. He digs through his backpack and pulls out the piece of paper with Mom's decrypted note. He flips it over, and we stare at the face of a boy.

"I bet this is a missing kid. They must not have milk cartons so they put pictures on flyers and hand them out in the marketplace."

"Do you think Double-Wide's in on it?" I wrap one braid clockwise around my neck. "And Madam Isis? No wonder she acted so strange when I asked about my dad. She must have recognized the name."

Gordy sits there, flipping his worn cards from one hand to the other. Finally, he breaks his silence. "Faisal warned us when we first met him that it wasn't safe for kids to be exploring alone. He must have known kids from Petra have been disappearing."

I realize finding Dad's things made me forget what I was doing. I have so many questions that my brain is buzzing from one to another without stopping. This must be how Gordy feels all the time. The questions just have to wait. Mom is in danger. She needs me.

"We gotta go." I tuck the key from the briefcase into my Moroccan pouch with the cord and hang it around my neck. I take out my journal to place the Valentine heart and newspaper clipping inside. I can't decide what to do with the passports, so I put them back into the hiding place in Dad's briefcase, back under the counter.

Gordy and I put on the jalabiyas. I look at him. He looks like Gordy in a dress. I probably look like me in a dress. Not what Dad would call an effective disguise.

"Wait, we can't go like this." I take a deep breath and go into the kitchen. I return with a six-inch butcher knife and instructions.

Gordy launches into a thousand questions, ending with, "Are you sure?"

"Yes."

"One hundred percent sure?" He holds the knife blade near my head.

"Yes." A wave of dizziness almost sends me to the floor.

"You don't act sure." Gordy twists one of my braids around his fist.

"Don't question, just cut." I brace myself for pain. Hair is dead anyway. It can't hurt, can it?

"I was thinking you couldn't glue it back on."

"I know!" Mom won't be thrilled, but Dad would understand because it is necessary. Necessary for our survival.

"You could just wear a dish towel."

"It's too hot," I say through clenched teeth.

"I'd think about it if I were you."

"You're not me. Get chopping."

I hate Gordy always second-guessing decisions, and now he's trying to make me do it. I don't want to think about it. The more

153

he questions me, the more I see Mom sitting patiently braiding row after row of little braids, adding a bright colored clip to the end of each of them. I loved hearing the sound of the clips as they clicked around my head every time I wiggled.

The sharp blade slices through my thick hair. The first bundle drops. Then the second. Then I hear 'oops'.

"What do you mean oops?"

"Well, it's not like I'm trained at this."

My fingers search for the ends of my hair, bouncing above my shoulders. I shake the remnants of my hair free and reach into my subway bag for a mirror. It's small, so I have to hold it out at arm's length just to see my head. The wispy ends curl up and around and back down. After all these years of wearing it long and braided I had forgotten about the natural curl. One side is shorter than the other, making me lopsided.

"You look very nice." Gordy takes two quick steps back.

I bend down and grab a handful of my missing hair. Wrapping a hair band around it, I secure it before stuffing it into the bottom of my backpack. I let loose a great sigh and for some reason feel a little better. At least I'm breathing again.

"Start coloring." I hand him the fat black markers from the bottom of my pack. When he's finished, I do Gordy. I stand back and admire my handiwork. His hair is dark, except for a few blond spikes I missed. I decided to line his eyebrows to match, which could be a mistake. They stand out on his face like angry caterpillars. Satisfied with our instant disguises, I figure it's time for us to get out of the souq before someone finds us.

A DECEPTION AND
A CONFESSION

We are like salmon trying to swim upstream in the Siq. I press myself into the rock walls to avoid getting stepped on by a donkey. Even though it's early afternoon, the tourists and their guides are headed back to their hotels to soak their feet and relax in cool pools sipping fancy drinks with paper umbrellas. I wish we were going with them. But first we have to find Mom.

"Remember the carved face along the Monastery steps?"

"You mean the Grumpy God?" Gordy says.

"We need to check it out again."

"What? Back up there? I thought we were going to see the Winged Lions."

"We are. But I have a hunch about those faces." I grab Gordy's hand and dodge between two donkeys determined to mow over or eat whatever is in front of them. Everyone seems to be leaving Petra, and I don't want to lose Gordy.

"You're going to read his lips?" Gordy starts making blah-blah sounds.

"Very funny," I say pressing ahead. "There was Nabatean writing beneath it. I think it might be a clue."

Weaving in and out of groups of people, I feel like I'm towing Gordy. I turn back to tell him to keep up, but the words die in my mouth.

Mr. Hasan has Gordy by the arm. Before I can react, he grabs mine. He says something in Arabic, all I know is he's angry. My brain rips through a dozen possible stories, none true, and none good enough, but it doesn't matter because my tongue is dead. Mr. Hasan isn't waiting for an answer. He flings us downhill in the direction of the hotel, and into the flow of the tourists.

I stop Gordy. I'm afraid to turn and show my face, but I don't want to go this direction.

"*Yella*," Mr. Hasan says cuffing Gordy on the back of the head to keep him moving.

Gordy and I dart among the tourists away from Mr. Hasan, who is now shouting in English, telling people to hurry. He doesn't sound or look as slick as he did when I first met him. He looks worried. Around a bend, we press against the rocks, letting the traffic stream by.

"He didn't recognize us," I say, my tongue jarred free by running.

158

"I think it's my eyebrows that threw him off." Gordy makes the caterpillars dance on his forehead.

Snickering, we walk all the way back to the gates, where a guard slams it shut after us and locks it. Then he lowers a painted sign until it rests right in front of us. Closed. All tours canceled.

"Now what do we do?" Gordy says.

I press against the metal, but my head is too big to fit through the slatted opening. I figure that means the rest of me won't go through either. Kind of like a cat. Mr. Hasan is on the other side of the gate, talking to a group of guards. I hear the all-too-familiar click clack, as Double-Wide appears by his side. Mr. Hasan points up the path toward the hidden entrance by the Treasury and then our direction. He looks past us, like he doesn't see us, before looking up at the sky. He is either very angry or something has gone wrong.

"I was thinking he's forming a search party for us," Gordy says.

"Maybe. We have to find another way in and make sure no one sees us, especially Double-Wide." Dad's handwritten note with the count of missing kids fills my thoughts. I don't want to add to the count.

"But this is the way in," Gordy says.

"We can use the back way, the path from the Palace Tomb to the hotel." Gordy makes a face. I know he's thinking about the dead man, just like me. We had a string of bad luck in that area. The djinn must hang out there. But this time, thanks to our disguises, maybe they won't recognize us either.

We climb for an hour, backtracking twice before I locate the correct cairns. While taking a rest at the House of Dorotheus, I notice a shrine carved into rock. That makes three we've found. I try to remember how many Faisal said there were, but my head feels dull from the thick still air. Sweat runs off me even though the sun has disappeared. I study the gray clouds positioning themselves on top of the red mountains, making them look alive and dangerous. I hope this is not an omen.

No one else is on the trail; even the Bedouin have vanished. I explain to Gordy again about the camel-back pattern for the trail, but he doesn't see it. When we reach the Palace Tomb, I hesitate. I want to see the shrine again, to sketch it, but I shudder at the thought of what else might be inside. Instead I lead Gordy down into the wadi. I run, knowing any eyes hidden among the rocks will be watching us. Dad's Rule Number 8: you are never truly alone.

Once across, I take the path back up into the mountain, following the long neck of the camel.

"I thought we're going to the Temple of the Winged Lions," Gordy says, pointing back down at the wadi. "You're going the wrong way."

"No I'm not. I want to see something else first," I keep climbing.

I don't answer Gordy's one hundred questions until we reach the shrine of the grumpy god.

"Faisal said there are twelve of these." I sketch the warrior-god's face on a fresh page in my journal. I also copy all the odd bits of carvings at the base, certain these are ancient letters. I wish I'd sketched the shrine at the House of Dorotheus. "Let's try to find another."

"But I thought we were going to the Temple of the Winged Lions," Gordy says.

I look down the mountain and can see the small form of the temple. My legs want to go downhill, but something strong in my gut tells me the shrines are important. "The grumpy god says shrines first."

"Really?" Gordy's eyes flash to the big lips, like he expects to see them move.

Having already checked near the Monastery a day ago, we go in a different direction. Gordy and I explore side paths, one by one, some no wider than a foot, carved by donkeys winding down the mountain. At least I spend my time searching. Gordy keeps stopping and picking up stray paper littering the trail, shoving them in his backpack. "Who appointed you garbage collector?"

"'Uzza," Gordy says.

I laugh at the idea she might also be the environmental goddess.

On one of the wider paths, we are rewarded with a tomb flanked by what is left of carved lions on either side of the doorway. Next to it is a second tomb where we discover a shrine carved into the red rock wall. There is more cursive writing. I trace the shapes in the air with my finger before copying them in detail into my journal. I sense that the shrines will lead me to Mom. Will they also lead me to Dad? That would be the best treasure if I could find both of them, together, alive, just waiting for me.

Picking up speed, we follow the path further south, along a high ledge overlooking the wadi. We come upon another group of tombs cut into the rock. A sign identifies the largest one as the Unfinished Tomb. Here, we find a shrine with two faces carved inside one box. Twins. I make a quick sketch, but I feel like I'm not any closer to understanding what they mean. My head's pounding, but the feeling in my gut tells me to keep going. We follow the path down into the wadi, along the street with the columns. We race across the exposed area, knowing we could easily be seen from the main trails. What if Mr. Hasan spots us and grabs us before we can find the Golden Girdle? I'll never get Mom back. Gloom presses down on me, and the mountains close in. I feel small and scared. The sky is dark and threatening. It smells like it might rain, even though it seems too hot for water to make it from the clouds down to earth. With my eyes on the sky, I stumble on a rock. Gordy catches me, and for a moment I stare into his bright eyes, one half hidden behind permanent black marker bangs. I'm glad he's here.

"Let's stop and drink some water," Gordy suggests.

We sit on the doorstep of Uneishu's Tomb marked with another shrine, emptying our water bottles. While guzzling water, I notice two fish carved on the lintel over the door. They swim in my vision with each throb of my head. I draw a diagram in my journal, marking where we found all the shrines. I play around with the writing I copied, using the code wheel, but the letters don't spell out anything that looks like the key to the Golden Girdle.

Gordy treats each clue like a rock, picking it up, describing it, and turning it over to examine all sides before discarding it. He's thinking again.

"What did the fax say?"

The fax. Doesn't Gordy forget anything? I search for what to say that wouldn't hurt his feelings. "You know how you kind of protected the crab disk by taking it?"

"Yeah."

"Well, I kind of protected this trip by grabbing a fax off my mom's machine at home and flushing it down the toilet."

"What did it say?"

"That the trip was cancelled, we weren't supposed to come."

"So you didn't tell anyone? Not even my mother?"

"No." I can't bear to meet Gordy's eyes. He must think I'm scum to lie to his mom.

Gordy doesn't say anything.

"If we didn't come, who'd help my mom and Faisal?" I say. "Dad always told me to trust my gut."

Seconds blow by like sand in the air. Gordy keeps gazing out over the wadi, his magic marker eyebrows pulled together.

"Why don't you like my mother?" he asks after a while.

"You wouldn't understand."

"Understand what?" Gordy's voice sounding tight, his fingers fiddle with the playing cards.

"I know it's not your mom's fault mine hasn't been around. It's just that she's here. Acting like she's my mom, telling me what to do, when to eat, when to change my clothes. Every time she does something Mom should be doing, it hurts."

Gordy keeps staring out into the wadi. He must be thinking how stupid I was to believe that a mother could just quit caring about her kid.

"I'm sorry I was mean to her, and you."

The ache in my head lightens and lifts. I hand Gordy my journal as a peace offering. He takes it only after I insist. He seems so distant, not even looking at my sketch of the shrine locations. To get his attention, I draw an arc, connecting the shrines on the Monastery side of the wadi. On our side, there is a second arc. It makes a broken circle, with the wadi cutting it in half. I draw "You are Here" and an arrow pointing to 'Uneishu's Tomb.

"Does anything pop out at you?" I ask, trying to sound hopeful.

Gordy's gaze is on the wadi below us. "I was thinking your mother said the Nabatean Pantheon will be revealed from the top of the Monastery, but what if she meant we'd see the Pantheon when we looked down."

My pencil connects the two arcs, making a complete circle. "What do you mean?"

"We know the Grumpy God is al-Qaum." Gordy points at the dot on my sketch that's at the top of the circle. "He's part of the pantheon."

"The shrines are the pantheon?"

"Faisal said there are twelve," Gordy says.

My eyes focus on the "You are here" arrow. It's pointing at 'Uneishu's Tomb. I extend the line until it intersects with the center point of the circle: the Temple of the Winged Lions. I snap my journal closed. "Gordy, you're brilliant. Let's go."

Map of the Shrines

DOROTHEOS SHRINE

UNIESHU SHRINE

AL-QAUM SHRINE

TEMPLE OF THE WINGED LIONS

UNFINISHED SHRINE,

A MAP AND A KEY

"Where are we going?" Gordy races after me on the steep trail.

"It's time for the Temple of the Winged Lions. The heart of the Pantheon, where the zodiac is."

When we retrace our steps back through the wadi, along the column-lined road, Gordy points at the ground. "That should make the gods and goddesses happy."

I follow Gordy's finger and notice the dried up riverbed moving. There's a ribbon of water flowing down the length of the wadi.

"It must be raining on the other side of the mountain. Maybe it'll bring us good luck."

We climb the steps to the raised temple, or what's left of it. The Temple of the Winged Lions is nothing like the description in the museum. The grand winged lions that used to guard its entrance have broken wings, damaged in an earthquake thousands of years ago. The entire front of the temple is ruined, leaving behind a rough block of a building jutting out from the wadi floor.

On a stone platform in the center of the temple is the statue of the lady holding the circular stone high above her head like an offering to the gods. Her face has been worn away, and her nose is missing. She has stumps where her angel wings would have been. I climb up on the platform and run my fingers across the crab, a man with horns, a bull and the twins of Gemini before I realize Gordy's talking to me.

"What?" I'm inviting a storm of questions and theories and thinking, but maybe he has an idea.

"All the great constellations live very long since stars can't alter physics."

"You should drink more water."

Gordy jumps up on the stone platform with me. "*All* is for Aries."

I pause for a moment when his meaning hits me. The zodiac mnemonic. In the top spot of the zodiac is the man with curved horns. Aries.

A chill runs through me even though the air is hot. "*The* is for Taurus, the bull." It should be in the one o'clock position, to the right of Aries. Instead it's to the left, in the eleven o'clock position. "Remember at the museum when you thought they messed up the order of the zodiac because the stars were in different positions back then?"

"Yeah. Stars do move in sky you know. The North Star's in a different position, depending on the season—"

"But they don't switch positions. On this zodiac, they've traded places."

Gordy points at the zodiac in the ten o'clock position. "*Great* for Gemini, that's the twins, right?" Gordy says.

I nod. The carving of two people in pointed hats belongs at two o'clock.

"So they just got the mnemonic backwards?" Gordy says.

I study it a bit more. "When they reached six o'clock, which is Virgo, they returned to the top and went clockwise. These two fish, that's Pisces. It should be located next to Aries in the one o'clock position, if it was all meant to be backwards. But it's placed here next to Virgo in the five o'clock position."

Gordy laughs. "You said *I* couldn't follow a map. They have their celestial map confused."

I gasp. "This is so simple; I can't believe explorers didn't figure this out ages ago. The order is messed up on purpose. The zodiac has twelve symbols. Faisal told us the old stories say there are twelve shrines, and look—" I sit down and open my journal to the page with the sketch of the shrines. "—they're carved in a circular pattern in the mountains around us. The zodiac is a map of Petra, not the stars."

Then I pull out the glossy picture of the zodiac. I cut the circle out and center it on my sketch, with the Temple of the Winged Lions being the center point.

"Aries is the warrior god, like al-Qaum. If I line up the zodiac Aries with al-Qaum, look where the Gemini twins point." In my sketchbook, Gemini is almost perfectly aligned with my drawing of the shrine with two faces. On my knees now, I turn to face the direction of al-Qaum's shrine, looking up through the open roof of the temple. "If al-Qaum or Aries is in the twelve o'clock position, then Gemini should be in the ten o'clock position." I rotate and am facing the mountainous area where we found the Unfinished Tomb with the two-faced shrine. I run my finger along the circle of my sketch to the Uneishu's Tomb. "There are two fish carved on the entryway. That's the sign of Pisces." I rotate again so that I'm facing six o'clock. Across the wadi I see the sign pointing to the path leading to Uneishu's Tomb. My excitement grows as the zodiac signs line up with shrines on paper and on the ground.

"Mom sent us to the Monastery with the picture of the zodiac so we'd have a hawk's eye view of Petra and so that we could see the layout and use the zodiac to guide us to 'Uzza's shrine."

"What did she mean with that part about the heart being the key?" Gordy asks.

"I don't know. But 'Uzza is represented by lions. Her shrine has to be over there." I turn around and aim toward eight o'clock, the position of Leo on the zodiac.

"That's...uh...tall."

Gordy's right. I'm facing the highest mountain on the west side of the wadi. It doesn't come to a rounded point like most of the mountains in Petra. Instead it's flat, unnaturally flat, like someone sawed it off.

I dig around in my backpack and find the map of Petra. I trace out the path from the Colonnade Street back behind the Treasury. The path zigzags on the map and stops at the top of a flat mountain. "It's the High Place of the Sacrifice. Sacrifice? What kind of sacrifice?"

Gordy doesn't respond.

He's straddling the statue and has his hand over the two o'clock position. The crab. Gold glints in his hand.

"What are you're doing?"

Gordy pulls back, and the golden disk is covering the carved crab. "It's weird. It kind of locked into place, like it was made to fit the carving. Give me the lion disk."

I take it out of the cloth wrapping that also holds the two half disks and the lion disk. "I want these back when you're finished."

Gordy places the lion on Leo.

I stand up with the two gold pieces in my hand. They are twice the size of the other disks. The right size for the center of the zodiac? I hand them to Gordy and hold my breath. I don't know what I am expecting to happen, but nothing does.

Then Gordy presses down hard.

CRACK.

The stone mouth of Winged Nike opens two inches.

I reach in slowly, hoping Nike doesn't bite. I remove a round object attached to a golden chain. Holding it by the chain, I see gold surrounding a bright blue circle with a black dot centered inside.

It's an eyeball.

"Uzza's eyeball," Gordy and I say together in awe.

RUNNING WADI AND HOPPING DJINN

The golden amulet dangles before my eyes. "Tomb Robber was looking for this." Dead Tomb Robber. I get a chill and force myself to turn off my overactive imagination.

"Can an eyeball be a key?" Gordy pokes at the golden ball, making it swing back and forth.

I don't answer because I see we have another raging problem.

I walk to the steps leading down from the raised temple. The sand is threaded with growing streams of water. The temple is now an island.

Flashes of lightening streak down on the mountains to the west.

"The gods don't seem happy," Gordy says.

Above us the sky is black. A cool breeze sweeps through the rocks. I glance up and watch heavy clouds parting and reforming above us, as if trying to decide when and where to fight. If it starts to rain hard, we could be in trouble. The water will run down into the wadi. Mr. Hasan said the wadi flooded sometimes. Twice in his life. I have no idea how old he is, but even if he was 100, I still don't like the odds. I close my eyes, turn my head skyward and offer a prayer to 'Uzza. Please help us. Please help us find the Golden Girdle fast because it'll lead me to my mom. In exchange I promise to make all fifth graders study Nabatean history, or at least all fifth graders I know.

"Look!" Gordy pulls on my sleeve. I open my eyes. A ray of sun slices through the clouds and casts a beam of light. The light beam sweeps across the mountain, from al-Qaum's shrine counterclockwise past Taurus, the Twins, across the wadi and coming to a rest on a flat mountaintop.

I know a sign when I see one.

"We have to climb," I say. I put 'Uzza's eyeball in the pouch hanging around my neck, next to the key from Dad's briefcase. I sling my backpack strap over one shoulder. Gordy retrieves the golden disks and puts them into his pack. We walk to the entrance of the temple.

"You mean wade." Gordy tests the depth and his sneakers sink into the sandy water.

At first the going is easy, with water pooling around our ankles. We splash from column to column, our jalabiyas soaked, holding hands for stability. Before we can cross the wadi half way, the water is up to my knees, pushing me off course. It's not raining. Where's the water coming from? I look sideways at Gordy and catch sight of rivulets of black running down the side of his head. I guess permanent markers aren't so permanent on hair.

I'm about to make a joke when Gordy slips, his head disappearing under the water. The jerk of his hand draws me down with him. I struggle to regain my footing in the shifting sand, but the force of the water drags me under. I burst through the surface to grab a breath of air and realize Gordy is still under water. I yank, and he pops up, sputtering and gasping for air.

"Can't...swim..." he manages before submerging again.

I try to double my grip by using both hands but before I can grab onto him, something collars me...or my backpack. I feel it being wrenched from my shoulder. The loose strap has caught on a signpost for a first aid station. It snares me while the now roaring river pulls Gordy away, his hand slipping from my grasp. I can't stay with my pack or I'll lose Gordy. Everything that's left of Dad is in there: my journal, my pencils, and my camera with the pictures of our last trip as a family. All my memories of Dad.

Gordy's hand slips along my palm and our fingers catch as the last and final link. I'm going to lose him too.

I slip out of my pack and stay with Gordy.

Together we surge down the wadi. I scream at Gordy to hold his head above water. He's fighting me as much as the water. My arm feels as though it is going to rip off. My legs, trapped in the folds of the jalabiya, only let me push up, to keep us both above water, but not to stop us from being washed away.

A djinn block saves us. The water throws us up against the large stone. I just know all my bones will break. If it's a door to the dead like Faisal said, this one is locked at the moment. I thank 'Uzza for that. The blocks, spread out along the wadi floor, refuse to move, standing firm, forcing the water to move around them. We are swept behind the block, and the water slows. We're in an eddy. Scratched, bruised, waterlogged but otherwise alive, I stand up, hauling Gordy with me. With our backs to the stone block we catch our breath.

"We need to climb up on it." My voice is hoarse from screaming.

Gordy nods, but doesn't climb. I bend over and tell him to use me as a step. Once he's up, he stretches out on his stomach and extends a hand. I no longer feel my arms, but somehow Gordy grabs them both and pulls. His face contorts, but he says nothing. I flop over the top, like a fish out of water and lie on my back, trying to breathe and calm my racing heart.

"Thanks," Gordy says. I can barely hear him above the roar of the river.

I gasp for air. "Remind me later that I hate you." I'm thinking about my lost backpack. Every last thing my father gave me. The clues from my mother. The newspaper article with the notes from my dad. The paper heart I had made for him. My house key, my money, my passport. Everything. Gone. Gone for good.

The roar of the water won't let me lie there. I roll over and gaze down into the river. It's not receding, but inching higher every minute. The djinn have offered us a temporary escape.

"We have to move again. How about a game of leap frog?" Four feet from our stone perch is another djinn block. On the other side, a third block juts up, still in the water, but closer to dry land. I tear off my jalabiya to free my legs. It's tattered now, after being tossed around in the wadi, dirty from the water and stained from my not-so-permanent hair color.

"Follow me!" I get a running start, or at least as much as I can while standing on top of a narrow rock. I leap. I fly through the air and discover something. The long jump is a lot like soccer; it's a lot harder than it looks. I know because I miss.

A BRIEF PAYMENT
AND A FALSE DOOR

My upper body lands with a thud on the next djinn block, but my feet dangle over the side. There is nothing to grab onto. My fingers dig into the sandstone, but they cannot keep me from slipping once again into the surging water. I drive my elbows down, trying to ignore the feeling of sandpaper ripping at my skin.

"ARRRGGGGGRHHH."

It's Gordy, on the rock, pulling me to safety. He must have leapt clear over me. I can't believe it.

"Next time let me go first." Gordy hauls me up, and then like a mountain goat in a bunched up jalabiya, he springs from one stone to the next one.

This time I jump harder. I fly through the air, landing hard and teetering on the edge. Gordy steadies me before I fall off the far side. There's a fourth djinn block hiding behind our current perch. We step down on it and hop onto dry land. Our water journey has taken us downstream. We have to backtrack to a trail that cuts through the stone theatre and leads up back toward the Treasury and the Siq entrance.

We walk, side by side, leaving a watery trail. Gordy's shoulders are slumped. "I'm supposed to remind you that you hate me."

"I lost my backpack trying to keep your head above water." How can I explain to him I feel like I have lost an arm or a leg? My journal can never be replaced.

"I never learned to swim," Gordy says.

I expect Gordy to start giving me percentages of how many Americans don't know how to swim, but he doesn't. When he's silent for way too long, I begin to worry his brain might have gotten water logged.

"You can have my deck of cards."

Surprised, I turn and see drops of water flowing down his cheek, but that could be from his hair, which has assumed its normal color.

"How about an offering to my queenliness of some food and water?" I fail to get Gordy to smile.

We approach the area near the Theater, where donkeys and guides gather. The place is empty, including the concession stand. The owner left in a hurry, not bothering to lock up. Gordy opens an ancient refrigerated display case and throws me a bottle of water. Cold water. I twist off the top and guzzle, remembering too late that my wallet is in my backpack. I stop and the water splashes down my face before I can right the bottle.

"Do you have any money?" I ask Gordy after searching my jeans pocket.

Gordy shakes his head as he empties his bottle.

"I guess we could leave an IOU." My last colored pencil is swimming with Nabatean fish.

"I have an idea." Gordy dumps out the contents of his backpack. I'm amazed. His stuff is dry, including the trash. The backpack must be waterproof. From the jumble of items, Gordy pulls out a shrink-wrapped package containing six pairs of boy's underwear and puts it on the counter on top of the empty water bottle. "Payment enough?"

I giggle, imagining the shopkeeper's face when he finds the package. Do Bedouin even wear tighty whities?

"You know, these are high quality briefs. It says one-hundred percent cotton. I was thinking that should cover some chocolate too," Gordy says. "Candy bar?" Without waiting for a reply, he tosses me one.

I rip off the wrapper and shove the entire bar into my mouth. I have never tasted anything this good. The chocolate is warm and melts in my mouth. I finish mine and beg for another. Gordy doesn't seem to hear me, his eyes fixed on a photograph of his mother. I catch myself thinking, not only do they not look like each other they are completely different. Gordy with is bright, warm eyes, always wanting to be a part of the fun. Mrs. Brown's eyes are like steel, cold and penetrating. His expression tempts me to ask what he's thinking. Maybe her don't-mess-with-me expression scares him too.

SPLAT. SPLAT-SPLAT.

The rain zeros in on us.

We both look back at the raging river. Without speaking, we gather up our stuff and follow a sign to the trail leading to the High Place of the Sacrifice. "Trail" is an exaggeration. Before us hundreds of steps spiral up and around the base of the mountain. We climb. The water makes the steps slick, and soon a small waterfall cascades down between my feet. I concentrate on one step at a time. I wish I hadn't lost my hat because the rain pelting my face makes searching for 'Uzza's shrine difficult. When we come to a side trail, we stop and explore. One trail takes us around to the wadi side of the mountain. I look for the djinn blocks. The water has risen; only the tallest stone sticks out above the surface. We'll need to keep moving to stay above it.

"When did you meet my mother?" Gordy says out of the blue.

"Your mom? Umm...at the memorial service."

"Your father's memorial service?"

"Yeah, she came up to Mom and me and said she was a friend of Dad's."

"You never heard of her before?"

"No, but there were lots of people I hadn't met before. Why?"

"When did she become your nanny?"

Gordy is wearing his laughing camel hat pulled low over his eyes so I can't see them. "Like you don't know. Three weeks ago, a week before Mom came here."

"Right. And when was your mother's article published? Before or after your father died?"

What an odd question. I round the trail to get out of the pelting rain before I answer. "Before. But I don't believe he's dead. They lied to me for some reason. He's here, or at least was here." Doing what? Why'd he have three passports hidden away? It's only a matter of time before Gordy asks me about the passports. Or where Mom got the gold piece for the zodiac? He doesn't forget anything. What can I say that doesn't sound weird? That my parents have secret lives that they lie about?

But Gordy's the one acting weird. Maybe almost drowning has short-circuited his brain. He starts to run along the path, slipping and sliding every few steps. I follow, but much slower, because I don't feel like breaking my neck. I catch up to him in front of a shrine. I wonder how he found it when I realize the trail ends at the shrine.

"Do you think this is it?" I say. It resembles the others, a face carved into the rock, but this face is stern and frowning, not how I imagined 'Uzza.

"I was thinking we should say 'abracadabra' and maybe the shrine will just open?"

I smile. Gordy's okay.

Despite the rain, my bruised body and a nagging feeling in my stomach that I'm missing something, I sense we're close. We check the face of the mountain for an opening, backtracking several times in case we overlooked it. When that fails, we return to the shrine, and I take the chain and the eyeball from the pouch around my neck. I dangle 'Uzza's eye in front of me, seeking inspiration.

"A sign about now would help," I shout to the storm clouds. Thunder claps, more rain falls. I hope that wasn't my sign.

It's a dead end. I slide down the rock wall across from the shrine. We've come this far. Quitting isn't an option.

"I was thinking we have the wrong shrine. We could go back and climb higher. Maybe 'Uzza would want her hiding place up high since she's also the sky goddess—" Gordy says.

"Goddess of the Heavens. Not sky."

I crouch down to study the script under the face. Despite the erosion, I can see letters carved into the rock: a little X with a broken foot, the Y on its side, a backwards P. I study the markings, lost in thoughts of shapes grouping and regrouping, hoping a pattern might emerge and reveal 'Uzza's secret. Gordy says my name twice before he gets my attention, and only because he calls me Anatolia.

"Don't call me that."

"But it's your name, isn't it? It sounds kind of mysterious you know, like Anatolia, goddess of—"

"Don't ever call me that or I won't be your friend anymore. I hate that Mom named me after a long gone civilization in Turkey. It doesn't even matter that I was born there. A normal person would have named her baby Helen or Troy, after its queen or biggest city."

"It could be worse," Gordy says with a slow grin.

"Impossible."

"She could have named you Turkey."

"I'll make stuffing out of you." I lunge toward him. Gordy jumps to avoid me, but slips on a wet rock and lands hard on his butt against the wall under the shrine. When he rolls back toward me, he is holding two rocks the size of Madam Isis's crystal ball.

"It's a false wall."

It takes me a second to understand what Gordy's talking about. There's a small hole in the wall under the shrine. Gordy pries another rock loose, and the hole enlarges. I drop to my knees and start pulling out rocks. In minutes we have opened a square breach big enough for us to crawl through. Gordy grabs his flashlight from his backpack and shines the light through the opening. We bump heads both trying to look at once.

"Go ahead. What do you see?" I sit up and rub the side of my head. My body is feeling abused. The last thing I need is a second concussion.

"A small room, or tomb, or something. Small."

"Anything inside? Like shiny? Or moving?"

"What?" Gordy backs out smacking his head on the stone.

"I mean like scorpions, not djinn."

"It's empty. We both could squeeze in, if we can get through the gap. Double-Wide wouldn't fit."

Just when I was starting to forget about that over-sized monster. Why'd Gordy have to bring him up now? "Move aside," I say. "I'll go first."

I twist, and I squirm, coaxing my shoulders in bit by bit. Once in, I use my hands as feet and walk, dragging my legs inside. I come to a stop when my head hits the wall. Gordy was right about small. I curl up and rotate on my butt so I can get the flashlight from Gordy's disembodied hand stretching inside the chamber. I flash the beam around and confirm Gordy's information. No jewels. No creepy-crawlies.

Gordy wiggles in so I flatten myself against the wall to give him some space. There's barely room for either one of us to move. I have a momentary panic attack, remembering being locked in the crate. But this time I resist the urge to kick and

186

scream because I don't want to knock any rocks loose that might be hiding scorpions. Gordy folds his knees tight to his chest and wraps his arms around them to give me some space. That's when I notice the second shrine. It's like the one outside, but the lines are cut sharp and the features clear. It hasn't been eroded by hundreds of years of wind, rain and curious fingers. This face of 'Uzza is beyond stern, with a godly-touch-and-die expression. The eyes are gouged deep into the stone, making them feel like they could pierce right into me. I run my hands inside the carved eyes and nose of 'Uzza. What has she witnessed all these years?

"Let me see." Gordy squirms around me. I hold the gold version of 'Uzza's eye, dangling from its chain. Am I supposed to return the eye to her? The words from my mom's note play over and over in my head.

Follow the map to 'Uzza's lost shrine. Find the Golden Girdle and me.

I press the eye into the right socket but nothing happens. It falls out of the carved indent unless I hold it there.

"What are you doing?" Gordy shifts his weight, pushing me up against 'Uzza.

"Wait." I reach across to the left socket and press in the amulet again. I cup my hand, expecting it to roll back at me, but the eyeball locks into place. Sand starts to pour from the eye, like tears I cannot stop. I scratch at the amulet, trying to retrieve it.

I'm pretty sure this isn't what should happen. I'm going to lose the eyeball and the hope of ever finding Mom.

The sand pours onto my feet, and I realize it's coming from multiple holes in the wall. The chamber begins to fill so fast I panic. "It's a trap. We have to get out."

Gordy flails about, kicking sand and hits me hard in the back. Then he stops. The sound of his voice scares me more than his words.

"We can't."

A QUEEN'S CURSE
AND A SAND BATH

The sand pours in faster than the water flooding the wadi. I try to pull the amulet out of the eye, but it has vanished into the wall, just like we'll soon disappear into the sand. It reaches our waists. It weighs us down; our arms are the only parts we can still move.

"It's the curse," Gordy yells.

Sand between our teeth. That's what 'Uzza promised to treasure hunters not worthy of uncovering her horde. I close my eyes and see Mom. She's wearing her favorite work clothes, khaki pants and a T-shirt, restoring some ancient treasure. I remember how excited she became when she spoke about the Nabateans. She danced around the room, reading the invitation from the Royal Ministry of Antiquities to come to Jordan and put together a traveling exhibit. If we could locate Queen Huldu's treasure, everyone in the world would be excited and want to learn more about the Nabateans. It would be the greatest discovery since King Tut. Mom believed when people explore their histories and connections to ancient civilizations, they learn a little about themselves.

I think about the mysterious package she left and the clues that got us here. I don't understand what I've done wrong. 'Uzza should be welcoming me, not drowning me in sand. I've let Mom down. She'll never know I followed her instructions, not because I want to discover the Golden Girdle, but because I need to find her. To make our family a family again.

"Ana, I have to tell you something. She's—"

I'd forgotten about Gordy, even though he is pressed up against me. The desperation in his voice makes me feel even worse. If it weren't for me, he wouldn't be locked in this box of sand. He believed me when I told him I was Queen Huldu's descendent, and the curse couldn't touch me. How wrong could I be?

"I'm sorry, Gordy, for—"

" —not my real mother—"

" —believing 'Uzza and Queen Huldu would protect me." The sand streams over my shoulders. "I must accept her punishment."

I push myself forward, flat against the rock and taste the sand between my teeth. It fills my eyes, my ears, and my mouth. My palms on stone, I accept my fate.

Found treasures
and Lost hope

I push forward, and the djinn's door to the dead opens.

I fall.

Sand swirls around me. Stone scrapes against me. My life passes before me.

I hit bottom. Literally. I am sitting on a stone floor. I still have Gordy's flashlight in my hand, which makes me wonder if dead people are allowed to take stuff with them. The light still works, illuminating a large chamber. The walls are carved with animals and Nabatean writing. Large pottery urns are piled in one corner. Along the back wall, stone shelves are filled with drinking cups, made of metal and encrusted with jewels. Then I see a stone altar. On it rests a crown, a dagger, and a belt. The glint in the flashlight beam reveals their golden gleam. Red, blue and white jewels burn bright.

My legs wobble as I stand. I approach the altar and kneel. This hurts my knees. If I'm dead, I shouldn't be in pain, right now. I shouldn't be able to feel anything. I reach out my hand to press my forefinger against the metal. But I stop. What if it all goes poof because it's just a dream? Or what if something bad happens, like it's the doorbell to the gates of hell? Why is it right here in front of me, and not hidden? But if I'm dead already, why would it matter? I shake my head and give the dagger a firm poke. It moves, but nothing else does. No fire bursts between my feet. I touch it again. It moves again. Only then do I accept what my eyes tell me. Before me is the Golden Girdle, the Queen's diadem and her dagger. I've fallen into the hidden treasury of Queen Huldu. The Horde of the Golden Girdle.

I hang my head in silence and offer a prayer. Thank you 'Uzza. Once I find Mom, she'll decide the best way to honor the Nabateans. Queen Huldu will be known by everyone and be more famous than King Tut, or even Elvis. Thank you for trusting Gordy and me.

"Gordy?" I twist around. Where is he? He was right next to me in the sand.

"GORDY!"

My words echo off the stone.

"GOOOORDYYYYYY."

Nothing.

I fling myself down onto the floor and wail. Gordy didn't make it out...that means...he didn't make it out. Gordy's death is too big a thought for my brain. It couldn't be true. I reject it. Gordy's a fighter. He saved my life in the Palace Tomb, and he risked falling to save me on the djinn blocks, like a true friend. A friend. Tears stream down my face. I see Gordy in his laughing camel hat grinning at my jokes. And all his thinking. I haven't had a real friend in a long time. How dare he not follow me? It's not fair. I'm the leader, and he's supposed to follow. But Gordy's like that, both sides of a coin. Skinny white legs, but able to jump like a goat. Never been on a trip, but ready to take up the quest to find the Golden Girdle. And now I've uncovered it, and he's not here. I'll never have the chance to ask him why he keeps a package of brand new underwear in his backpack and where did he buy such a cool waterproof pack and...and...why is he scared of his mother?

"GOOOORRRRRDDDDDYYYYY!"

Silence.

Then sobs.

They come from somewhere deep and don't want to stop. I cry for everything I've lost: Dad, Mom, my journal, my colored pencils, my tattered jalabiya, but most of all, my friend Gordy. This was our adventure. At first I thought it was mine, but I know I would never have gotten this far without Gordy.

The light from Gordy's flashlight flickers. I turn it off to save the battery and huddle in the darkness. Is this what Gordy feels right now? I shiver even though it's not cold. The aloneness slices through me. The total darkness—

Or not.

I lift my head. It should be total darkness. Light penetrates the chamber from behind the terracotta urns. I wipe my cheeks and make myself get up. I shove one of the urns, and something inside sloshes. Behind the urn, I find a small hole, square-shaped, that looks like it was put there for a purpose. I drop to my knees and peer through.

Large spotlights—the kind archaeologists use when excavating in deep pits—shine far below me. People push wheelbarrows. Others are digging. I've never seen an excavation with this many workers. It's like a giant ant farm.

As my eyes adjust to the light, I make out more details. The workers aren't small just because they're far away. They're kids. They've been working a long time, judging by the filth of their jalabiyas. Dad taught me the importance of paying attention to what you see and what you don't. In this case what you don't hear. No one's talking. The only sounds are shovels moving dirt, the occasional clank of metal against metal and the hum of the generators.

I shift, trying to see where the wheelbarrows are going. Some people are sitting in chairs, but the angle is too steep for me to recognize much other than shapes. I look the other direction and notice the rock walls, smoothed and rounded. It's a large cavern, the uneven curves of the walls cut by the ancient river that flowed through the wadi.

"*Wajat shyy,*" a lone voice calls out. The boy sounds tired and scared.

There's a blur of movement. The kids form a circle around someone in the large pit. The people in the chairs are moving too. The one in a well-worn canvas hat and khaki pants strides across the cavern floor and starts climbing down a ladder. Once he reaches the bottom, the circle breaks open to let him through. He kneels next to a boy. It's quiet now. I can hear an occasional scraping sound. The boy must have found something in the dirt. Minutes tick away. My knees hurt from the hard stone floor.

A sudden movement draws my attention back down. The workers in the circle cry out and scatter. A large man raises a shovel and hollers in Arabic, causing all the others in the pit to move away. I don't understand what he's saying, but I recognize the voice. It's Double-Wide. The well-worn canvas hat drops to his knees next to the pit, motioning to someone down below. The hat slips to one side, and a flash of long blonde hair tumbles free. The pale skin is visible even from a distance. Double-Wide throws the shovel at the boy, ordering him to dig. Before the boy bends down, he glances up in my direction.

It's the face of Faisal.

These are the missing children.

The one in the hat and khaki pants isn't a man at all.

"Mom?" I whisper in horror.

POLYGONS AND SPHERES

I fall backward, gasping at what I've just witnessed. I can't breathe. I careen into one of the urns, making it teeter on its narrow base. It rocks one way and then the other, crashing over onto the stone floor. It shatters, reverberating off the wall, like hundreds of breaking pots. A strong smelling liquid splashes across the stone floor and wall.

I'm shaking from head to toe. I don't believe this. My eyes must be playing tricks. Mom wouldn't hurt a kid. She wouldn't steal artifacts. She wouldn't...would she?

But how do I explain the gold key? Where did she get it? Why didn't she tell anyone about it? Was it because she didn't need it? Or me. That's why she abandoned me. She's working with them to steal Nabatean history? Is this what the dead Tomb Robber meant by my thieving mother? Mr. Hasan was assisting her to get rid of me so she could plunder with no interruption? Is that why she sent me on a wild goose chase after the Golden Girdle? But I did find it. It wasn't just a legend or a diversion.

I cradle my head in my hands. My brain is drowning. "It can't be Mom," I groan. They've done something to her. There has to be an explanation. I've lost Gordy. I've lost Dad. I can't lose Mom too. I don't want to think about what I saw. Those poor kids. And Faisal. Did he know my Mom's involved? Is that why he acted so strange? Once again I feel like Gordy, jumbled thoughts roll around in my head, except nothing is making sense no matter how hard I think.

"Poor Faisal." He was afraid for Gordy and me. He warned us, to help us get away. I've messed up everything. Gordy would be alive if I hadn't led him into a trap. At least I can help Faisal.

I turn my flashlight on and stare up at the ceiling where I fell through. In the wall, where it meets the ceiling, there's a cylinder-shaped stone. I study the outlines of a rectangular piece that rests on top of the cylinder and continues into the wall. Polygons and spheres. Could it be a lever and a fulcrum? I slide over to the wall and run my feet through the sand. Enough to fill maybe four sandbags. That's a lot of weight. I consider the fulcrum again. Gordy and I stood on the stone above. Our weight alone wasn't enough to move the stone. When the sand poured in, the weight increased. But the floor didn't tilt until the chamber was almost full. I wrack my brain. A lever needs a shift of weight to work, like a seesaw with weight at either end.

I gasp. When I decided we were doomed, I leaned against the shrine. That must have triggered the lever, causing the stone to drop on my side, and spilling the sand and me down here. If the sand streamed down with me, but not Gordy, it is possible… just maybe that Gordy remained on the other side, alive.

I have to find out. I can't go back the way I came in. If the Nabateans used levers to open their doors, there must be another lever in this chamber and another door. I flash my light around the walls. I don't find any cylindrical stones. Then again I didn't see the other one when standing on top of it. Think.

I run my hands along the chamber walls, feeling for breaks. When I touch something sticky, I pull my hand back. The liquid from the urn is gummy and smells like the stuff Dad drank in the evenings, but worse. It has discolored the yellow stone, making the wall appear bloody. Gross. I decide to skip this section but stop. The gooey liquid at my feet is still moving, red lumps inching along the stone floor and disappearing into the base of the wall.

The exit.

How do I open it? If a lever operates it, it'll need weight to make it work. I jump up and down on the floor before the crimson wall. Nothing happens. I lean against the wall. I just get sticky.

Maybe the weight of one person isn't enough. I grab the top of one of the urns and push and shove until it rests in front of the wet wall. I hear an odd sound, of stone hitting stone. I duck, expecting something to fall down on me again. But nothing tumbles from above. I glare at the invisible door.

"Open Sesame," I say, just for the heck of it.

When neither Queen Huldu or 'Uzza answer me, I decide to stick with the weight theory. I go back to the stone altar. I stare at the Golden Girdle with a mixture of awe and hatred. It's the one thing Mom wants. I could pretend I never saw it. But I can't.

I cinch it around my waist under my T-shirt. I'm surprised by its lightness; the tiny golden links seem more like thread than metal. The cold against my skin tells me otherwise. I eye the dagger. I might need it to hold off Double-Wide. I thread the jeweled handle into one of the belt loops at my jeans, I can feel the dagger rub against the side of my thigh, but the handle stays locked in its holster. For a moment, I feel like a swashbuckling pirate. I resist the urge to set the Queen's crown on my head. I figure taking all three of her treasures might bring bad luck. Instead I place the crown, which is as heavy as it looks with all those walnut-sized gems, on a stone shelf alongside the metal drinking cups.

The stone altar is now empty. Wrestling it over to the wall is even harder than moving the jugs of liquid. I push and pull and rock and roll, but it doesn't want to move. I put all my weight into one final effort, but my feet lose their traction in the goopy liquid, and I fall back into the bloody wall with a thud.

The stone revolves and to my surprise I am propelled around to the outside of the chamber. An ancient revolving door.

I try to close my mind to thoughts of Mom and what I'll say to her. As I head down the corridor, I feel what it means to be alone. The stone pathway winds around and merges with another passageway, and a series of steps. Do I go up or down? Faisal is below me, but where could Gordy be if he escaped the sand? Outside, wandering about? Mom's down too. My gut says down. "I'm coming to save you Faisal," I say to the rock walls.

I hear Gordy in my head debating the pros and cons about whom to save first. He'd decide to head to the cavern first, because he'd be thinking there's no proof that he, Gordy, is alive, but Faisal may not be alive for much longer. When I reach step 200, I rest and calculate. The steps measure between four and six inches. I've gone down about 80 feet. I estimate the bottom of the cavern to be twice that deep. I keep going. Other chambers open off the staircase, but they are empty. I wonder if tomb robbers, like my mom, have emptied them. Just thinking that fills me with shame. How could she, after all she told me about how wrong it is to plunder from archeological sites? There just has to be another explanation. Mom wouldn't do any of these things. She couldn't. Could she?

I climb down another 280 steps before I reach the end of the passage. I must be close to the cavern. The passage used to go on, but is now blocked by rubble. Is this a sign? Should I turn back and look for Gordy? I know what Gordy would be thinking. I pull out a stone and then another. Maybe I can clear a hole big enough to squeeze through. I grab a rock sticking out about chest high and tug. It starts a small avalanche of debris, causing a lot of noise.

I jump back and listen for an alert. I can hear voices. They sound like they are coming from the other side of the rubble. I choose my rocks with care now, pulling them out one by one. I feel like an archaeologist, removing one layer of dirt at a time in order to reveal a story. The story I want to uncover is who's on the other side. I should make a plan, but my instincts tell me to keep tunneling.

BREAD CRUMBS AND
CREEPY GUARDS

I dislodge a rock the size of my head and peer through. Before me is the skeleton of a forgotten city. Carved archways and doorways. Red cobblestone streets that have been cut and pieced by hand, one at a time. Dark entrances that lead into what were once homes and businesses. And a familiar sound.

Gordy.

He is alive, and he's here!

At first it sounds like he's talking to someone, but his voice is the only one I hear. I roll another rock out of the way to create an opening large enough to squeeze through. It's tight but I have to get to the other side. I don't think about the scratches from the sharp edges or my fears that the rubble might collapse and trap me. I focus on Gordy. He's here, breathing, talking, and alive...and singing?

On the other side, I rock the stones back, so nothing looks out of place. I work my way down the street, ducking inside the abandoned shells of buildings while listening for sounds of danger. The coast is clear. I continue to track Gordy's voice, the words indistinguishable, but melodic. I want to yell out to him, but what if he's singing to someone? And why? He sounds close. I spring into a stone opening in the wall, ready to greet him. It's empty, the ceiling so high I can't see it. Sounds are bouncing off the walls. I go back outside. His voice is coming at me from all directions. How will I find him in this echo chamber?

That's when I notice a playing card on the ground. A dusty boot print covers the Queen of Hearts. I stop to pick it up and spot another, a little further away. Bread crumbs. Gordy's version of a trail marker.

I follow the sound and the cards into a cave like space, empty except for a light radiating from a hole in the ground. The light shifts in a continuous circle. I move closer. The singing echoes up from the pit.

"*And the rockets' red glare, the bombs bursting in air—*"

I peer over the edge.

"*—went poof through the night that our flag was still there—*"

"Gordy?"

"Ana?"

I've never been so happy to see anyone in my whole life. I'd bear hug him if he wasn't down in a hole. But he's not sitting

204

still. Every few seconds, he makes a quarter turn, shining a light up and down the wall and then repeating the motion again. He's like a robot with jammed programming.

"What are you doing down there?"

"Double-Wide dumped me here. *Oh say does the star-strangled banner do wave—*"

"Double-Wide?" My eyes sweep the chamber. It's empty except for Gordy. "Why are you singing?"

"You said to make noise."

"Well you got the words wrong. Gave proof through the night."

"*Over the land of the free and the home of the brave.*"

Gordy's lost it, gone mental. I have to get him out of there.

"Try and reach my hand." I lie face down in the dirt and slither toward the edge. "I'll help you out."

"STOP."

"Why?" I pull back.

Gordy turns another quarter turn, the light flashing up and down. "Scorpions."

"Where!?" I jump to my feet.

"Everywhere. The holes in the walls are filled with them."

I stare at the walls. Nothing wiggles, but I'm not taking any chances with a motel for creepy crawlies. I scoot away from the ledge. "I don't see them." I flush hot, wondering if Gordy is playing with me.

"Scorpions are very sensitive, you said. That's why I'm singing."

"Huh?"

"I just want them to feel relaxed. They sting you know."

I shudder and scoot back more. "I noticed a ladder in one of the other rooms. Don't move. I'll be right back."

I don't wait for Gordy to respond, but race back down the cobblestone road. In the second room, I find the ladder, one of those heavy-duty metal ones archeologists use for scaffolding. It is three times as long as I am tall, and heavy. I can't lift it, so I step inside the first rung and drag it behind me. I don't get very far before I'm winded. At this rate, it'll take all day. Gordy doesn't have all day. I doubt he has another five minutes before he's the catch of the day.

"Oh say can you see by the dancer's light—"

The feet of the ladder have left a trail in the dirt behind me. I drop the ladder and rub out any markings. I do this six more times before I reach Gordy. His flashlight lets off a softer glow, as the battery slowly dies. I slide it the rest of the way over the pit and then tip the ladder down toward Gordy. He just sits there at the bottom.

"Well, aren't you going to climb up?"

"I need your help. My hands are tied together. I can't hold onto the ladder and the flashlight."

I grip the top of the ladder. There are scorpions down there. I hate scorpions. Creepy crawly bugs that can hurt you. Lots of them. I'm sure the djinn are punishing me for raiding Queen Huldu's treasure. Maybe they feel I'm not worthy. Mom owns an enamel scorpion given to her by an anthropologist friend. She sometimes pins a scarf with it for museum events. She told me the scorpion was important in Pre-Islamic Art, both as the embodiment of evil and as a protective force. I know it isn't real, but I have a hard time hugging her when that thing is attached to her. These scorpions aren't enamel. They're deadly to people, dogs and probably djinn.

The darkness is swallowing Gordy, but I hear him loud and clear as he continues to mess up the words of America's First Song. I have to do something before the scorpions think it is night and go searching for snacks. I take a deep breath and decide as long as I continue moving; nothing can attach itself to me. I free Queen Huldu's dagger from its jeans holder and clasp the blade between my teeth. The movies make this look easy; it's not. I shimmy down the ladder until I bump against Gordy. His eyes grow wide when he sees the curved blade, but he keeps singing. One slice of the thousand-year-old blade cuts through the cord binding Gordy's hands. The problem is me.

I'm blocking the light from reaching the wall behind me. The scorpions' snappers and tails *click-clack* as they scuttle among each other. The walls come alive as they continue their quest for food.

"Move it," I scream at Gordy. I press the dagger into his hand in exchange for the flashlight. I zigzag the beam, blinding the scorpions. Then I shove up against Gordy pushing him upwards. I follow right behind him, unable to resist a glance behind me. Big mistake. Scorpions now fill the space where Gordy once sat, and a solid trail is scurrying up the legs of the ladder behind us. The noise vibrates around me.

Click-clack.

Click-clack.

Snip-snap.

The feeling something is crawling on me overcomes me. Their hard spiny legs, their pinchers. I shake my body hard as I continue to climb.

Gordy makes it to the top, rotates onto his side, and reaches down to help me. "Ana. Don't move."

"They're coming!" I grab for the dirt above me, chunks of the pit dropping around me.

"Freeze!" Gordy blocks my way. He leans down past me, and I hear a whistle and a crunch. The Queen's dagger swings up past my head with several skewered scorpions on board. In one swift motion, I propel myself past Gordy and to the safety of the ledge. I roll to the ground to crush anything else that might have hopped on for a free ride, my shirt sliding up in the process.

"You found the treasure."

I see Gordy staring at me, the Golden Girdle gleams in the soft light. I whip my shirt down, still checking for scorpions. When I'm sure there aren't any, I realize Gordy is still staring at my waist. "When 'Uzza's stone shifted, I tumbled into the treasury and Queen Huldu's stash. All of it."

"Wish I had your luck. I fell into a guardroom with Double-Wide and his goons. That's all you took?"

"And that." I motion to the dagger in Gordy's hand. "The treasure's not ours to keep. I only took them because I thought I could use them to save—" The steady click-clacking distracts me.

The first scorpions are making it to the top of the ladder. Gordy reaches over and gives the ladder a hard shake, then pitches it to the other side of the pit.

"Let's go."

Gordy walks toward the opening and stoops to pick up his backpack, thrown behind some rocks. He's lucky; he hasn't lost everything important to him. That's when I remember the cards I had stashed in my pocket. I hand them back to Gordy. He seems pleased I found them.

"I found Faisal and the missing kids," I blurt out. "We've got to save them from Double-Wide and his boss...I saw her and..." I can't say 'Mom'. I still don't want to accept she's involved with people who steal children and antiquities.

"I know." Gordy hangs his head. "I figured it out too but didn't know how to tell you." Gordy points to the pit, "It's okay if you hate me."

"Hate you? You're all I have. Now let's find Faisal."

Exposed Lies
and High Waters

Finding the cavern isn't difficult. The sound of metal scraping against rock echoes and pings around us like a homing device, guiding us in. The bigger problem is what to do once we get in there? Gordy and I are no match against Double-Wide and the other guards stationed around the dig site. Gordy is listing our options for rescue mission: surprise, frontal attack, a fake out…Half of me is soothed to hear him thinking; the other half is worried about Mom. How could I have missed seeing her cruel side? I had no idea that Mom's lie detector was just one of her special skills. But murder? I still can't believe it. This was a trap all along. She used Mr. Hasan and her silly clues to make me think she was in trouble, when all she wanted was to get rid of me.

I stop when I hear shouting and the heavy scraping of something coming from the other side of a carved doorway.

Then, Gordy and I slide forward and crane our heads around the corner. A corridor with steps leads down and broadens as it enters the mouth of the cavern. All I can see are the backs of the guards and workers as they focus their attention on something in the excavation pit. I slide my body along the cave wall. I need an idea, and I need it now. The wall glistens. I run my fingers along it and feel water trickle through tiny cracks. Under my fingers the cracks widen as the stone crumbles. It's as if someone switched on a garden hose, full force, and it's eroding the wall from the other side. My brain snaps back to struggling in the current with Gordy.

"We have to warn them," I whisper to Gordy, but he's not there.

Gordy's leaping down the last of twenty stone steps to the cavern floor. His shouts echo like sparks off a flint stone.

"You're a liar. It was always about the treasure. That's why he was looking for you. It's why you killed him. I'm not going to let you get away with it." He swings around in front of Mom and charges, dagger extended.

Mom just stands there, her back toward me. Gordy waves the dagger at her, his face contorted with rage. "You're a cheater and a fake."

With cobra speed, Mom grabs the jeweled blade from his hand. "Where did you find this?" she says in a strange voice.

Gordy fights to retrieve the dagger, but she holds it up, the curved blade skyward, out of his reach. The harsh light from the excavation lamps glints off Queen Huldu's dagger, sending reflections of reds, greens and blues spiraling around her. Mom begins to change in front of me, laughing as Gordy is pulled away by Double-Wide. He locks Gordy's hands behind his back, while pushing him hard to the ground. Then he kicks Gordy in the back for good measure. I hear a cracking sound, not sure if it's coming from Gordy or the walls. Gordy curses both of them between sobs of pain and defeat.

"Leave him alone," I scream. I run toward her. "I have what you want." I raise my shirt, the Golden Girdle strapped around my belly.

She turns to face me for the first time.

I freeze.

Her long blonde curls sweep across her face and frame steel blue eyes.

"Mrs. Brown?"

"Ana?" Mom's voice rings out. A hand reaches up from the pit below me, grasping the sides of a ladder. Then a blonde head and a thin body emerge. "Ana!"

"Mom?" I see her crawling up from the excavation pit, lunging, arms reaching for me. Her clothes are filthy, her face pale and lined, black circles under her eyes. The rest of her words are lost in the sound of boulders crashing somewhere behind me.

Mrs. Brown lurches forward to block Mom while trying to yank the Golden Girdle from around my waist. But Mom's wrapping her arms around me. I'm pushed and pulled as they struggle over me. Mom fights like a crazy woman, kneeing and clawing and biting but I feel her strength failing. I hold on to Mom. I'm never letting go or doubting her again.

The cavern wall disintegrates, and water gushes in, boulders thundering, water roaring. It's like a truck plowing into the side of my body. My arms and legs lock around Mom before she is washed off her feet. The surging water sends us down and under as it pours into the excavation pit. I kick my legs hard to stay afloat. One of the guards floats by and grabs on to us. He pushes on Mom's head, trying to keep himself above the water. Mom struggles. I am afraid she'll lose me and be dragged away by the current. His weight draws us under. I latch on to his handlebar mustache and yank until I see panic in his eyes. His hands break loose. He drifts down and away. I haul Mom back to the surface.

The surge has slowed to a steady stream of water. Large holes in the cave wall have opened, filling the pit and turning the cavern into a huge swimming pool, growing deeper by the minute. Mom fights against sinking, her kicks growing weaker with each stroke. I tell her to roll over on her back. I hook my arm under her chin and swim against the current toward the partially submerged stone staircase. I search for Gordy among the kids clinging to the rock wall. Others flounder in the water.

"Shewf," I holler to them to look at me. I lay on my back, holding Mom's hand, as we do the back float. They form a human chain, floating on their backs, and kicking.

Just as I think we are going to be okay, the last of the lights go out and the cavern plunges into darkness. Screams fill the blackness. Dad's Rule Number 9: technology will always let you down.

"Don't panic." Mom's voice is faint but firm. "The water must have shorted out the generators. We need to swim toward the rocks on the left side. There are emergency lanterns there."

Together we stroke, fighting the current, as it tries to trap us inside the swirling eye at the center of the pool. When I feel rocks scrape against my legs, I try to find a handhold. Instead, many hands reach for me and pull up. Mom comes with me because I'm never letting her go. A small blue light flames in a metal cage. Gordy's holding the lantern.

"You can't swim," I say.

"Faisal saved me."

"Where is he?"

Gordy points toward the back of the cavern. There's a splash near a floating chain of kids. Faisal breaks through the surface with a small girl.

"Faisal!"

"Okay Miss Ana. Yes?" Faisal drags a sputtering girl behind him.

"You can swim?"

"Uncle learn me in hotel pool at night."

"We have to get everyone out of here, before we're trapped."

"One way out." Faisal points back toward the stone staircase, only three steps remain above water.

Mom sits on the rocks with the lantern to light our way. I jump back in to the dark waters. Faisal and I gather the chain of kids and swim for all we're worth toward the entrance to the cavern as the rising water threatens to cover it. We return a second time for Gordy and the kids clinging to the rocks. One by one, we pull them to the dry passageway. Mom stays on the rocks and holds the light until the last one is out. The water begins to fill the corridor leading up to the ruined city. By the time we get the last two kids out, the water has climbed so high our heads touch the rock ceiling. Gordy helps us pull them to dry land. I do one final check of the water for any stragglers as I go back for Mom. I see two heads bobbing by the back wall. Definitely not kids. Maybe two of the guards? I'm not sure what happened to Mrs. Brown. The water starts to swallow me.

I grab Mom's hand. "Take a big breath and kick hard." We dive down to the flooded corridor, stroking with all our strength against the current. Losing direction in pitch black is easy, but we keep our faces into the current, as it guides us along the ten-foot-underwater path to safety. Gordy is waiting for us, holding another emergency lantern. The blue flame sheds a lonely light on the streets of the hidden city, now taking on water. We splash through waist high water to catch up with Faisal who is moving everyone up the street toward the chamber where Gordy was trapped, frantically looking for another way out.

"It's a dead-end," Gordy yells.

"I came this way. There are stairs on the other side. We need to find the hole to the passageway," I say.

The water picks up speed as it swirls around us. I run my fingers along the stones until I find the rubble patch of the false wall. The hands of twenty-two kids make short work of the rocks, tearing away at them. Each time a stone drops, water pours through, lowering the level of the water around us.

"Faisal, just keep heading up the stairs. There must be another way out." Mom and I help the kids, one by one, dripping wet, shivering from fear and cold, into the hole. Faisal carries a small girl who has twisted her ankle in our escape. Gordy, Mom and I bring up the rear, with Mom in the middle, and Gordy and I helping her to climb.

"How did you find Queen Huldu's treasure?" Mom says.

My stomach clenches. With everything that's happened, this is the first thing she wants to know?

"Gordy and I followed your clues. The dagger's gone, but I still have the Golden Girdle." I lift my shirt so she can see it. She reaches out, running her fingers over the inlaid jewels, looking at it as though she has found a long lost friend. "It's okay. It's safe." I drop my shirt, hiding the treasure from sight. I don't want to talk about treasures; I want her just to want me.

We continue to climb, the water licking at our heels, but its pace has slowed. I count steps. When I hit 480 I show Mom the passageway to Queen Huldu's treasury. We don't stop even though we stumble and fight for each breath. There are another 300 steps before we come to a dead end. Faisal and the kids are removing rocks and threads of light tease them to work faster.

"It's a doorway, sealed in ancient times," Mom says upon examination.

When I step through the breach, I see a stone obelisk. A matching pillar towers at the other end of the flat-topped mountain.

"This is the High Place of Sacrifice," Mom says.

"Did they kill people here?" Gordy says.

"Animals mostly. As a way to appease the gods."

The heart of the storm has moved south. A softer rain is misting over us, leaving the rocks slippery and me wishing we were still in the cavern. Faisal gathers the kids together into a tight knot, huddled together against the wind and rain. I count by twos. Twenty-two including Faisal. They all made it out. I help Mom take a seat in the protection of a small outcropping of rocks. Her work clothes cling to her. She looks thin, like she hasn't eaten since she left home. I unhook the Golden Girdle from around my waist and hand it to her. It hurts to see the way she looks at it.

I turn away, reminding myself it's the reason why we came to Petra, our little adventure together, just like old times. It's over now. The water can't possibly come this high. We'll have to wait until someone rescues us or for it to all to drain away. I scan the wadi for signs of help. The Temple of the Winged Lions is almost submerged. The Monastery and the peak it rests on are obscured by white fluffy clouds while further downstream rain and the occasional lightning bolt attack the Petra mountains. The sun appears and disappears in intervals, the wind whipping the clouds into an angry dance, as if the gods are unsure about ending their fun and games. Only an insane person would be out in this weather. This makes me smile inside and look for Gordy.

He's sitting alone in the mouth of the passageway, staring at a waterlogged photo. I walk over and join him on the stone step. He's studying a picture of Mrs. Brown.

"I'm sorry about your mother." I don't know what else to say to someone who discovers his own parent is a criminal mastermind.

"She's not my mother. She just faked it to trick you and your mother into trusting her. All she wanted was the treasure," Gordy says through clenched teeth. "She used me. She never wanted to be my mother."

"Not your mother? Who…why…?"

"Tomb Robber…the dead one…he didn't have her picture by accident. He knew who she was."

"I don't understand. Tomb Robber had your mother's picture?"

"It's how I figured out what she was up to. She was the one behind your mother's disappearance and Tomb Robber's death."

"Maybe there's another explanation." I look over at Mom. "Sometimes things aren't as they seem. For a while, I thought it was my mom who was working with Double-Wide because…because—"

"Ana, you knew in your heart your mother wouldn't steal antiquities. I know Mrs. Brown would because her house is full of stolen things. Not just antiquities, but…me."

I'm about to say something to make him feel better when I hear a familiar sound.

Clack.

Clack.

Sacrifice and Death Plunge

Double-Wide holds me in a head lock. Mrs. Brown leers down at my upturned face with Queen Huldu's dagger pressed against my cheek.

"So Dr. Steppe. The jewels or your daughter. You decide," Mrs. Brown says.

I brace myself for a long standoff because Mom will never give up a treasure like this to a thief. Mom will be a tough negotiator to the end, making Mrs. Brown give up, just like the shopkeepers. I wait, but I don't hear anything. Instead I see Mom standing, water streaming down her face. Rain? Or is it tears?

She cradles the belt with outstretched arms. Mrs. Brown steps forward and snatches it. Then Mom reaches out to Double-Wide for me. I lurch, the knife forgotten, but only for the instant. Mrs. Brown points it instead at my heart.

"Sorry Doctor." She pushes Mom back. "We're not finished yet. There's an entire room of this stuff, and this one knows where it is."

"She's a child, leave her alone. I've done everything you've asked. I'll take you to Queen Huldu's treasure." Mom's hands are still outstretched.

Mrs. Brown nods toward Double-Wide. "When Drago here first told me the police were looking for a missing man by the name of Jack Steppe, I thought it was a stroke of divine fortune. Here was the man whose wife knows more about Nabatean artifacts than anyone in the world. Getting you here was easy with an offer of a traveling exhibition and then a ransom note waiting for you when you checked in at the hotel. You were so desperate to hang on to the hope the mysterious Mr. Steppe was still alive you believed we were holding him. *'I'll do anything to save him,'* you promised. Instead, you wasted my time. You had two weeks to show me the Queen's hiding place. Now it's your brat's turn. I'll bring her back safe and sound once she takes me to the hidden chamber."

"Don't trust her!" Gordy says. "She'll hurt you, like everyone else."

Mrs. Brown turns and slaps Gordy hard across the face. A bright red mark flares across his cheek.

"You second-hand piece of trash. You're lucky I came along and saved you from a life of endless foster homes. No one wants an eleven-year-old boy. I gave you a home, new clothes, a chance to travel the world. Were you appreciative? No! Instead, you betrayed me!" Spit shoots out of Mrs. Brown's mouth while she speaks. "Stay out of this if you know what's good for you."

"I won't lie for you anymore. You're not my mother. You're not even a good fake mother."

A look of disappointment washes over Mrs. Brown's face. "I liked you Gordon. I thought you could be an okay kid. That maybe, just maybe we could help each other out. It's hard not getting what you want, not getting what you need. You have the same hunger for more. I see it in your eyes." She lets the knife drop from my chest as she reaches out to him.

"I'm not like you." Gordy swings at her.

Mrs. Brown swats away Gordy's blow and bears over him, menacingly. "I asked one thing from you in return for my generosity. Watch the girl. Keep her away from the excavation site until I need her. You couldn't even do that right."

Gordy lunges at Mrs. Brown, this time a dynamite-packed body of rage. Double-Wide releases me and knocks Gordy to the ground again. But Gordy isn't finished. He kicks at Double-Wide's ankles. The massive beast loses his footing and buckles over. Gordy attacks again and the two struggle on the wet rock, as they slide toward the rocky ledge. This is my cue. I fly for the Golden Girdle and twist it out of Mrs. Brown's hand. Mom may have been willing to give it up in exchange for me, but I've worked too hard finding it to let it go now. I leap out of the way as Mrs. Brown slashes at me with the jeweled dagger and buckle it over my soaked shirt. Mom grabs at Mrs. Brown.

"Help me you idiot," Mrs. Brown cries searching for Double-Wide. But he cannot save her. I watch as the massive giant pleads with Gordy as he hangs head down over the edge. Like a turtle trapped on its back, he is frozen, unable to move, except for the heaving of his chest as great sobs escape. Gordy doesn't release him right away, but taunts him, pushing him a little further over before pulling him back. That's when it dawns on me; Double-Wide is afraid of heights. The entire scene must have freaked Mrs. Brown out a bit too, because for a moment she has forgotten I have the Golden Girdle.

Then she remembers.

I dart left, then right, looking for an escape. Mom blocks Mrs. Brown for a second time before taking a serious tumble in the rocks. I duck and weave around the obelisks. Mrs. Brown doesn't play fair. She anticipates my every move. She jabs when I pop around the obelisk, hitting the exact opposite of where I am expecting. The blade connects, slicing into my left arm. A stream of blood mixed with water travels down my arm. Mom screams. Mrs. Brown drives me backward. I stumble and fall into a pool of water. The metal plaque next to me reads: Sacrificial Basin Used by Nabatean Priests.

I feel a jolt of adrenalin. I refuse to be a sacrificial offering. That's not the deal I made with 'Uzza. I scramble on all fours and back down a smooth channel in the rock that slopes down and away from the killing stone. Mrs. Brown continues after me, her eyes wild and teeth exposed in a victorious sneer.

I have made a grave error. The channel is the drain the ancient architects designed to send the sacrificial blood over the edge of the precipice. Springing to my feet I see a sky set aflame by the sinking sun. I have nowhere to go.

"I have you now," Mrs. Brown says, crowing in triumph.

Movies always switch to slow motion in crash scenes or other moments of impending death. I always thought that was just Hollywood. Frame by frame, I watch Mrs. Brown reach for my waist. The dagger points between my eyes. As Mrs. Brown's fingers inch to my waist, two small fists pummel her like a punching bag. The dagger drops. Mrs. Brown slips. She grabs at the Golden Girdle. Gordy shoves her away and reaches for me. I tilt backwards away from Mrs. Brown. She claws at the air and locks her hand around the Golden Girdle. Together we fall.

We slide down the chute and off the ledge. Mrs. Brown releases me with a scream. I push hard against the rocks with my feet, propelling my body clear from the cliff, and out over swirling waters. I tuck into a cannon ball, plunging deep and kicking my feet hard when I hit bottom. When I burst back to the surface, it takes one breath before I know where I am. I stroke for the djinn blocks downstream. Mrs. Brown is bobbing nearby, but the current grabs her, and she disappears from my view. I float for a moment in the calm waters of the eddy before once again scaling the sandstone block. Over the gurgling of the water I hear the distinct sound of a helicopter.

MISSING KEY AND
KEEPING SECRETS

Bundled in white hotel towels, I snuggle between Mom and Gordy on a springy sofa. We're seated in the hotel lobby. A man in a jalabiya hands out steaming glasses of tea to our waterlogged group. The helicopter rescue must have been amazing as Faisal and the other kids recreate being snatched up into the air and flown to safety. My memory's playing tricks on me because all I can remember is one moment I am on a rock, and the next I'm wrapped in Mom's arms.

The police are here too. Lots of them. As well as Double-Wide. He's wearing handcuffs, not drinking tea. There's no sign of Mrs. Brown.

"Why isn't he in handcuffs?" I point at Mr. Hasan. "He was helping Mrs. Brown."

"No," the police chief says, "he was trying to help you. Mrs. Brown was attempting to blackmail him. He wanted to free Dr.

Steppe without creating an international scandal, but when you showed up, things got out of control."

"But he set Double-Wide on us," Gordy says from under his towel.

"Mr. Hasan arranged for the helicopter search. We knew you were inside Petra once we found your backpack in the wadi. We were very surprised to find you with twenty-two missing kids."

"Double-Wide?" Mom says. She sounds normal. I try not to notice the deep purple circles under her eyes and the taut skin. I can only imagine what she has been through the last three weeks.

I point to a handcuffed Double-Wide, whose real name we now know is Drago—which is almost as good a name for this goon. "Did he hurt you?"

Mom buries her head in my hair. "Yes," she says softly. "And he said he would kill your father if I didn't cooperate."

Tears stream down my cheeks. I feel so guilty I suspected her of being a thief and not caring about me.

"Did you see Dad?" I want to tell her I found his briefcase and ask her about all the passports, but worry it will just upset her even more.

"No. They said he was held in another location. I would see him as soon as they had the jewels."

"Maybe if I had been smarter and faster…figured out your clues right away…I could have found Dad—"

Mom silences me with a kiss. "You are amazing. I only wished to get the package safely out of Jordan before it was too late, I never expected you to locate the Golden Girdle or me. I hoped you'd understand I'd been kidnapped and call the police. I was afraid to say too much. Mr. Hassan promised he would help me, but I couldn't trust him. When I realized I had been brought here under false pretenses and he was in on it, I knew I could only depend on you for help."

"So you didn't send the fax telling me not to come?"

"No, Mr. Hasan must have. It wasn't until you arrived that he figured out Mrs. Brown and the woman stealing antiquities were one and the same." Mom hugs me a little tighter. "How could I have left you in the hands of that evil woman?"

"I took care of Mrs. Brown, but I still don't trust Mr. Hasan." I flare my nostrils in his direction. "But Dad? Is he really alive?"

Mom holds my face between her hands. "I don't know, baby." She kisses my forehead once more. "When did you cut your hair?" She says it as if she's seeing me for the first time.

I tell Mom about Madam Isis and meeting Tomb Robber, who turns out to be a Scottish art cop from the international police force INTERPOL. Then I explained how we dug up the other half of the gold piece, discovered the zodiac was a map, and found out that 'Uzza's eyeball amulet was a key. Gordy's blond hair and shining eyes emerge from under the thick towel,

229

and he interrupts to add details I'd forgotten. When I finish, Gordy tells both of us how he figured out what Mrs. Brown was up to.

"When Mrs. Brown offered to take me in as a foster kid, I thought she was doing it to help me, to give me a chance of living with a real family. She gave me new clothes and stuff, but she didn't do it for me. All she wanted was for me to help her steal."

Gordy looks down at the soggy playing cards in his hands, trying to shuffle the wet mess. "I promise you, I didn't know what she was doing at first. I was just supposed to spy on you, and tell her what you did. But when I found her picture in the envelope you pinched off Tomb Robber, I figured he was looking for her, and then he got killed. It was all lies. The only thing she cared about was finding this treasure. I think she tried to find clues in your home and when that didn't work, she had her goons kidnap you, Dr. Steppe. I couldn't let her hurt Ana so I stopped helping Mrs. Brown and helped Ana find you. I'm sorry. I should have told the truth, but then you'd know I lied too, that I was the imposter, and you would throw me away, like, like the piece of trash I am."

Gordy reaches into the backpack at his feet and places something hard and cold into my hand. "I was thinking it can't replace what you lost, but this knife is special. It's the one thing that's truly mine, besides my cards." Gordy holds up the limp pack. "You keep the knife. I don't think they'll let me have it in prison."

"Prison?" Mom and I say at the same time.

"For aiding a thief and murderer." Gordy slumps over, ready for his punishment.

"Gordy, the only place you're going is home with us. After that, we'll figure out what's next." Mom gives Gordy a kiss on his forehead, which makes his cheeks turn pink.

"Slap swear?" Gordy says. His face reminds me of how he looked when I said he could help Mom and me find the Golden Girdle. Except this time he launches himself at us, and we have a group hug on the sofa.

Wrapped safe in Mom's arms, I ask the next most important question. "What will happen to the Golden Girdle?"

"It's on its way to the Royal Museum in Amman," Mom says. "Along with the other artifacts you discovered, it will be catalogued, photographed and one day put on exhibit for the world to see."

"That means we've kept our slap swear promise to 'Uzza," Gordy says.

"Will we ever get to see it again?" I'm not sure how to ask my real question.

You two uncovered Huldu's treasure, and that makes you famous archeologists. I wouldn't be surprised if the King of Jordan himself doesn't offer you a reward."

I glance at Gordy. A reward? Maybe he was right after all; we'll get to keep something.

I hear a throat clear twice before we can untangle ourselves. A familiar man in a dark suit and tie is standing before us.

"Dr. Steppe?" Mr. Gray says. He looks just like he did in our living room in New York, standing with sad eyes, saying how sorry he was about Dad dying.

Mom nods.

"I'm sorry we meet again under such difficult circumstances. I've heard about the ordeal you and your family have been through, but I need to speak to you about your late husband."

"What is it?" Mom's voice is once again tired and strained.

"In private, I think best."

Mom shakes her head. "We've had enough secrets in our family, Mr. Gray. Say what you have to say."

Mr. Gray peers down at me with kind, but penetrating eyes, reminding me of my dad's.

"Your father was a friend and colleague, and I'm deeply saddened for your loss. My sympathies again to you and your mother. He was a great man, and he served our country with honor."

"Why are you here?" I demand.

Mr. Gray smiles. "You're a lot like your father. I'm looking for something he may have left behind."

Gordy squirms next to me but I keep my eyes on Mr. Gray. It's an odd name, rather like Mrs. Brown.

"Like what?" I flare my nostrils.

"A small key," Mr. Gray says.

"Your colleagues asked me about this key after the memorial service," Mom says. "I told you then I don't have it. My husband was a careful man and kept his secrets to himself."

Next to my beating heart I feel the Moroccan pouch Dad gave me. It burns against me and is heavy around my neck. Why would this strange man show up now and ask for a key?

"Don't you think you should be looking for my dad, not some key?"

Mr. Gray scrutinizes me. "I am hopeful we will be able to recover his body once these criminals tell us where they buried him."

Mrs. Brown said she was a friend of Dad's. I never met her before the memorial service, just like I never met Mr. Gray. She had a nice smile and penetrating eyes too. Everything that came out of her mouth was lies.

"How do you know Dad's dead?"

"We know."

"So when did he die?"

"I know this is very difficult to understand for a child—"

Mom's hand closes in on mine and squeezes.

"When and where did Dad die?" My eyes burn into him, my lie detector on full force.

Mr. Gray looks away. "Seven months ago, here in Petra. I'm sorry."

I stare at Mr. Gray, Faisal's words spinning in my head. *Faisal help Jack Steepp five moons ago... men still look for him last week like he is with living.*

"Your father was a very important man, and you must trust me, we looked very hard. But this key, did your father ever show you a small key? He might have worn it on a chain, or had a special hiding place for small things?"

I think about the fax, torn up, hidden and lied about because I believed Mom didn't want me. And Mom's secret package, which I hid from Gordy because I was afraid to trust him. I was wrong. Mom never stopped loving me, and Gordy turns out to be the best friend I've ever had. But Queen Huldu kept her secrets from tomb robbers until the time when they could be protected and honored by the world. What about Dad and his secrets? By hiding them from Mom and me, did it mean he didn't love us or want us? I know in my heart he did.

Thoughts swirl in my mind, the puzzle pieces falling into place, one by one. I hold the key that could lead me to Dad. Then I think of Dad's Rule Number 10.

I meet Mr. Gray's gaze. "No idea what you're talking about."

ARABIC AND NABATEAN VOCABULARY

Ashra   Arabic: ten

Djinn   Arabic: mischievous spirit (origin of the English genie).

Frankincense   An aromatic gum resin used as incense and in perfumes.

Huldu   Nabatean: Nabatean queen, married to Harith IV, who ruled Petra for 30 years (9 BC-40 AD).

Jalabiya   Arabic: a traditional Arab robe, normally ankle length, with wide sleeves and no collar.

Khalas   Arabic: enough, finished.

Khamza   Arabic: five.

Kibbeh   Arabic: Arab dish made of bulgur (crushed wheat) or rice and chopped meat, torpedo-shaped and fried.

Kiffiyah   Arabic: a traditional Arab headdress, a cotton cloth, often checkered.

Myrrh   An aromatic gum resin used as incense and in perfumes.

Shewf   Arabic: look!

Shukrun	Arabic: thank you.
Siq	Arabic: shaft; name of the entryway into Petra.
Souq	Arabic: an outdoor market.
Tayib	Arabic: good.
Wadi	Arabic: a dry riverbed.
Wajat shy	Arabic: I found something.
Yella	Arabic: Get going.

AUTHORS' NOTE

While *Lost in Petra* is a work of fiction, the Nabatean civilization did exist and was a major trading power during ancient times. A queen named Huldu lived in Petra in 9 BC; her face is on coins from the period. The names of the tombs in the story are real. Go to Petra and climb the steps to the High Place of the Sacrifice. It really is a long hike!

The Nabatean zodiac can be found today in the Cincinnati Museum, not in the Temple of the Winged Lions. The Grumpy God shrine is in the Temple of the Winged Lions, not on the path to the Monastery. The Map of the Gods exists only in our imagination.

Since Petra was rediscovered in 1812 by Swiss explorer Johann Burckhardt, archaeologists have been digging up its secrets, trying to learn more about the Nabatean people, and why Petra disappeared from history for over a thousand years. There is archaeological evidence of a major earthquake, which destroyed vast parts of the city, causing people to abandon them. While ancient texts talk about the wealth of the Nabateans, the Horde of the Golden Girdle is fictional...or at least we think it is. Who knows what treasures remain hidden in the red mountains.

CPSIA information can be obtained at www.ICGtesting.com
Printed in the USA
LVOW05s1542250713

344649LV00001B/188/P